Whit's End

Willow Spring Ranch
Laura Harner

Copyright © 2014 by Laura Harner

Cover photograph by DWS Photography

Cover Art by Laura Harner

Edited by Jae Ashley

All rights reserved.

Published in the United States by Hot Corner Press.

ISBN: 978-1-941841-15-0

Contact the publisher for further information: Hotcornerpress@gmail.com

Contents

Acknowledgements

The author acknowledges the trademarked status and trademark owners of the following trademarks mentioned in this work of fiction:

American Idol: FremantleMedia North America, Inc. Hummer

Chevy: General Motors, LLC

Corona: Cerveceria Modelo, S.A. de C.V.

Four Seasons: Four Seasons Hotels Limited

Jeep: Chrysler Group, LLC*Jim Beam*: Jim Beam Brands Co.

Les Paul: Gibson Guitar Corp.

Marlboro: Philip Morris USA Inc.

Marines: US Marine Corps, a component of the US Department of the Navy

McDonald's: McDonald's Corporation

SEALs: The Department of the Navy

Stetson: John B. Stetson Company

Technicolor: Technicolor Trademark Management SAS Corporation

Toyota Camry: Toyota Motor Corporation

Twitter: Twitter, Inc.

Wranglers: Wrangler Apparel Corp.

Chapter One

White-knuckling the steering wheel, Whit held his breath and gunned the big four-wheel drive Chevy, willing the beast to fight up the steep incline of the seasonal creek bed. The engine roared, and the front tires grabbed, inching him forward, closer to the flat ground he desperately needed if he was going to get out of here before the area became impassable. The front of the truck crested the bank, but the rear tires spun on the loose rocks of the arroyo and the bed of the truck slipped sideways. For a moment, Whit wondered if the truck was going to circle around and dump his ass in the wash. In this weather, it wouldn't be long before the normally dry creek would be roiling with flash flood water, rocks, and debris.

He babied the gas pedal, tapped the brakes, and jerked the wheel hard left. Every muscle tensed as he leaned into the turn as if he could move the truck to safety through sheer force. The truck inched forward with a groan that could be heard over the pounding rain. With a sudden jerk that snapped his neck, the front wheels grabbed and the truck shot forward, hurtling him toward the tall pinyon that marked the entry to his property.

Everything seemed to happen in slow motion as he braked too hard and the truck fishtailed, sliding inexorably toward the pine. He might have yelled as the sound of metal-meets-tree punctuated his impromptu parking job. *Well, fuck.*

With the driver's side door tucked up close and personal with the tree, Whit slid across to the passenger side and climbed out to assess the damage. Yesterday, like most days in Arizona, there hadn't been a cloud in the sky. But some funky spring storm that had been building over the Pacific coast caught a high wind, and overnight, the storm warnings had been raised to extreme. Word of the accompanying rains and flash floods had been enough for the Willow Springs Ranch owners to postpone the long-planned Ranch Quest set for this weekend. The twenty kids in treatment for life threatening or terminal illnesses might have been looking forward to spending the day at the WSR, but they would have to wait another week. If the rain came in the forecasted amounts, there would be no way to get a bus down the long dirt road that led to the ranch.

Which was why Whit was now out here at his newly purchased ranch land. As soon as his boss, Cass Cartwright, confirmed the delay of plans, Whit had beat feet to get to the ramshackle cabin set in the middle of his seventy acres. He'd made it before the rain and stayed just long enough to ensure the place was as secure as he could make it. The power generators were in the shed, the tools locked away, and the windows and doors were secured. The place might not be much, but it was his. He counted himself fortunate to find acreage close enough to the WSR that he could keep his job and still use his days off to work at making his cabin habitable. Someday he'd be able to build, but for now, this was his, and he planned to take damn good care of the place.

Without even looking at the damage, he already knew all hope of getting back to the WSR today was gone. The entry to his land was straight off the highway but the turnoff to the WSR was five miles back, toward the interstate, and even if he could see in this deluge, the dirt road to the ranch would be impassible by the time he extricated his truck.

After turning off the ignition, he jammed his hat down harder on his head, then pushed the door open, which turned off the truck lights, pitching him into an eerie gloom. His boots squelched in the mud when he jumped from the truck. Removing a coil of rope and a shovel from behind the seats and a flashlight from the glove box, he locked the truck and prepared to hike back the way he came to wait out the storm. At least he'd get a fair idea of whether or not his cabin was watertight.

Lights danced crazily across the trees in front of him, and for a moment, Whit thought he was seeing a strange lightning pattern refracted in the pouring rain. The lights bounced then swept to the left, and Whit turned to catch sight of a white sedan as it swerved, jerked sideways, then rolled to a stop not more than fifteen feet from his truck. The door opened and a man in boots, jeans, long-sleeved shirt, and a white hat jumped from the driver's side door. The outfit might be generic cowboy, but Whit had no difficulty recognizing the familiar figure as he jumped from the car, and the way he started running blindly said trouble.

"Hey, over here," Whit yelled, flipping on the flashlight and waving his arms, already moving in the man's direction. The man turned toward him, just as the predicted trouble arrived in the form of a black Jeep Wrangler.

The Jeep bounced over the drainage ditch to come to a stop next to the car. A bright light flashed once before the door opened and someone in a blue plastic rain poncho climbed out. The light flashed again, and he heard the man's voice call out, effectively putting the puzzle together for Whit.

"Brody! Mr. Kent! Keith Marker here from TYZ news. Any comment on Lisa's statement earlier today? Do you want to comment on the rumors you're ga—" He slipped in the mud and executed a perfect belly flop, landing camera first in a reddish brown puddle.

Country music superstar Brody Kent had been due to arrive at the Willow Springs this morning for a few days away from the fallout surrounding his three-day marriage to Lisa Bennington, an up-and-coming young actress. Whatever the true circumstances surrounding their whirlwind courtship, filing for an annulment after seventy-two hours had shifted the lovey-dovey wedding coverage into a vulture-like feeding frenzy. Apparently Brody had missed the WSR turnoff because this idiot reporter with a camera thought it was a good idea to use his Jeep to play a potentially deadly game of chase in hazardous weather.

Whit pulled his new houseguest behind him, rage at the reporter nearly hot enough to steam in the downpour. He knew exactly what question the reporter had been asking when he'd fallen. *Are you gay?* The questions regarding Brody's sexuality had been the top news story for days now. Because America didn't have anything more important to talk about. He might not be able to change the national conversation, but by god, this was *his* land now, and the least he could do was offer some protection. As soon as he could, he'd get Brody to the WSR, and then Cass could take over, but for now, he wasn't about to let this jerk run Brody Kent to ground so he could mount his head like a trophy.

"Get behind my truck," Whit shouted. He drew his gun from his holster, cocked the hammer of the big .45 by the time the reporter got to his feet, his front covered in mud. When he started to bend down to pick up his camera, Whit fired into the ground just to the left.

"You're trespassing. Get out or I'll shoot."

There might have been a few sputters, but under the circumstances—a gun pointing at his chest—the man climbed in his Jeep with ill-disguised anger, then rocked the wheels a few times before he stomped on the gas, spinning the four-wheel drive vehicle around, spraying mud everywhere.

Whit holstered his gun, then trotted over to where the journalist had fallen and pulled the abandoned camera from the muck and hung the strap over his shoulder before returning to his truck to retrieve Brody Kent.

"You okay?" he shouted. The white hat nodded, rain pouring off the brim, the face kept down, as if he had a sudden need to study his shoes.

"Okay. We can talk later." He looked toward the rapidly rising creek. Four hours earlier, the ground had been dry as desert, strewn with baseball-sized stones and easy enough to drive over, as long as you went slow. Now, at least two feet of water spilled and splashed, a precursor to the raging torrent that would leave them cut off for hours or even days, depending on how long the rain fell. And thanks to his own near catastrophe climbing the bank, this side of the crossing had turned into a mudslide and left a steep drop of six feet to the bottom.

There was little time to waste. Whit took the rope, looped it around a tree, then handed one end to Brody. He twisted the other end around his hand. "Do I need to tie this around your waist, or do you think you can hang on? I need you to anchor me while I cross, then I'll do the same for you. It's just enough to add some support, the water is moving fast and it's gonna hurt like hell if it knocks one of us on our ass."

"Where are we going?" Brody shouted. His gaze traveled from Whit's truck to the rapidly rising water.

"I've got a small cabin, back that way." Whit pointed across the creek to the barely visible dirt track that led deeper into his property. "It's not much, but it's shelter."

"Can't you get me to the Willow Springs Ranch? They're expecting me."

"Yeah, I know, I work there." Whit figured the reporter probably spooked the man—hell, he probably never traveled without a bodyguard or two. He was right to be cautious before going off into the woods with a stranger, but this was not the time to hesitate.

"Look, let's try this from the beginning." He offered a flash of a smile. "*Hello*. My name's Whit Truman." He watched to see if there was any flicker of recognition, but of course there wasn't. There wouldn't be, which was a damned shame, because something about this man got to him in a big way. Even standing here in the pouring rain, looking a whole lot like a drowned rat, and refusing to meet Whit's eyes, he was still sexy as hell.

Taking a quick breath, he sought to reassure the man. "I work for Cass Cartwright at the WSR. We can't get there in this weather, the roads are going to

15

be impassible soon, and my truck is down for the count. Let me get you someplace safe, then you can call Cass and let him know where you are. Now hold on to the rope, because if we stand here much longer, we're gonna ride out this storm from my truck—at least there's water and food at the cabin."

Whit turned and started to make his way toward the bank when a hand on his arm stopped him.

"I have to go to my car, I can't leave my stuff." Brody dropped the rope and turned away.

"Goddammit—" Whit shouted to the other man's retreating back. He had two choices. Run after the little shit and drag him across or... *Fuck*. He ran after the little shit, prepared to imitate a pack mule.

The man in front of him might have been four or five inches shorter than he was, but he traversed the distance quickly, despite the way his boots slipped and slid in the mud. Whit moved a little more cautiously. If one of them went down with a broken ankle, they'd be in even bigger trouble than they already were. He followed Brody to the trunk of the Toyota Camry, wondering why he'd picked a sedan made for city driving to come to the WSR. The ranch was at the ass-end of a dirt road, and although they very rarely experienced weather like this, any four-wheel drive vehicle would have been a smarter choice.

As if reading his mind, Brody shouted, "I sort of took off without telling anyone other than my manager and I asked the gal at the rental counter for something nondescript. He opened the driver's side door and reached in to hit the release button before joining Whit at the trunk.

Staring in dismay at the three large and two small suitcases, he turned to the smaller man. "Brody? We can't carry all these," he shouted over the sound of the thundering rain as it pounded off the car.

Brody pointed at one of the smaller bags. "I need that one," he shouted back. He turned away from Whit, as if dismissing the help, and walked around to the passenger side of the car.

Fuck. Well, at least it was small. And so what if Brody treated Whit like the help. That was exactly what he was. He'd have likely been carrying all the suitcases into the guest casita if they'd both been at the WSR—he might as well do it here, too.

Whit dropped the reporter's camera into the trunk. With no more time to stand around and debate, he hauled out the bag, slung the strap over his shoulder, and slammed the lid before Brody could decide he needed more.

"Come on, we've got to hurry."

Brody pulled a hard-sided guitar case from the passenger seat, then closed and locked the doors. He nodded, but with his hat pulled so low over his brow, all Whit could see was the grim line of his mouth. Seeing the guitar added an answer to the question Whit hadn't asked: what was so damned important that it wouldn't keep until after the storm?

Whit took the instrument case, and added the strap to the one already on his shoulder. He hesitated just for a moment before taking Brody's elbow, but for safety's sake, they needed to stay together and upright. He shortened his own long strides only slightly as he raced the two of them toward the creek. Reaching the rope, he assessed the change in the water flow, and tied the end of the rope to a tree that leaned over the creek. It would have been better if they could have brought the rope with them, but the water was moving too fast to take a chance.

He looked at Brody and waited. When Brody finally looked up, Whit's breath caught in his throat. He'd just wanted to make sure he had the other man's attention before he reviewed their plan—he hadn't counted on the effect of those eyes. It wasn't the first time he'd seen them up-close, but he'd thought he'd romanticized the effect they'd had on his teenaged libido. Now, despite the hat and the near darkness of the storm pressing down on them, his knees went a little weak. They were standing close enough that he could practically count the gold and black flecks that seemed to swirl in the light green pools. That was when something inside Whit's chest clenched tight.

The hair on the back of his neck raised, and Whit had a momentarily stupid fantasy that he'd been hit by Cupid's arrow. The notion evaporated instantly as with a tremendous crash of thunder, a bolt of lightning split an ancient juniper fifty feet on the other side of the wash. As the tree splintered and burst into flames, Brody twisted the rope around his forearm before gripping it tightly in both hands. He set his feet, and gave a curt nod. Despite having the rope tied to the pine behind him, he would still act as anchor.

Whit shifted the guitar case and bag so they rode more securely on his back, well above the level of the roiling water. Edging as far away from the mudslide as possible, he stepped onto one rocky outcropping, then another until he was knee deep in the tumbling water, the slick soles of his cowboy boots providing little in the way of traction on the slippery rocks. As soon as he reached the other side, he tied the rope to another sturdy pine and signaled to Brody to start across. With the rope now serving as a handhold, Whit made his way back toward the water, reaching Brody just as the man's boot slipped and he nearly went down. Instinctively, Whit shot his hand out and caught the waistband of Brody's jeans. He hauled him upright, then wrapped an arm around the smaller man's waist and together they emerged from the water. Brody limped badly, his right leg obviously injured.

"Got a ways to go," Whit shouted. "You okay?"

"I'll manage," Brody gritted out. "Give me one of those." He reached for the straps on Whit's shoulder, but he brushed the offer of help aside.

"I got these. You hang on to my arm and we'll get up the hill together." To his relief, Brody didn't argue, just gripped his elbow, lowered his head, and followed Whit's lead. It wasn't an easy hike, the steep incline made more treacherous for the water rushing downhill. They followed a game trail, and Whit kept his pace slow, scanning the path for any hazards, steering them toward the large granite slabs and away from the sandstone, which would be far slipperier in the wet.

After a long and difficult walk, they finally reached the plateau the previous owner had bulldozed for the homesite. According to the realtor, the former owner planned to build on the site and do most of the work himself, so he'd built a small cabin for temporary housing. Whatever house plans had existed hadn't come to fruition, but the former owner had added to his one room cabin over time. Whit's favorite feature was the large screened-in porch, which would be useful for three out of the four seasons. A bedroom had been added to the back of the cabin and a roughed in bathroom would make it very nice once the work was complete. A small but functional kitchen stuck out at an odd angle from the front room. Eventually, Whit intended to build a house of his own design, but this was adequate for the time he'd be spending here.

Brody's steps faltered, and Whit glanced down to catch a flash of a look cross the man's face. Dismay? Disappointment? It didn't matter. They were here, and he intended to get Brody Kent to safety.

"I…uh…" Brody hesitated, and Whit realized now that they'd arrived, Brody's nervousness about being caught alone in the woods by a madman had resurfaced. With no one around for miles and Brody in no shape to defend himself, he had an excellent point.

Whit looked down at Brody, who was steadfastly staring straight ahead, not meeting his gaze. All he wanted was to make the man feel safe, to get him into the shelter of the cabin. "I promise, I won't hurt you. You can call Cass as soon as we get inside."

Brody didn't say no, but he didn't step forward either.

Whit released his grip from around Brody's waist, then tucked his finger under the dimpled chin, urging the smaller man to look up. "Please," he said. "Let me help you."

Chapter Two

Brody Kent had never felt so wet, so helpless…or so frustrated. Calling Cass Cartwright for a place to escape had been the best decision he'd made in years. All Brody had wanted was a week or two, completely away from any cameras, away from any more stupid questions, and especially away from the greedy, conniving, lying bitch he'd married in a monumental fit of stupidity.

Brody's manager, Tim Fichter, had gone to great lengths to make the arrangements and swore there was no way he would be followed to the remote Willow Springs Ranch. Brody had taken a flight from LAX to Santa Barbara, then another to Prescott, with the idea the two smaller airports would make him harder to spot. Once in Arizona, he'd rented a car and driven the long way around to Kingman, before finally heading toward the WSR. He still didn't know how he'd been located.

Goddamn all this shit to hell, anyway. He was so fucking tired of it all. The damned idiot from TYZ could have gotten him killed.

The sad thing was, Brody couldn't even say for sure where he'd picked up the tail. He hadn't noticed the big black Jeep following him until he was on the isolated county road that was the last stretch between the interstate and the turnoff to the ranch. Brody's attention had been on the western sky and the black clouds moving inexorably toward him. The wind had picked up considerably, shooting tumbleweeds across the road with increasing frequency. Lightning flashed in the distance, jagged arrows searching targets on the ground, the thunder a long-delayed rumble, barely heard from inside the vehicle.

By the time the rain hit, he'd known he was in trouble. The completely ordinary sedan so carefully selected to avoid notice was no match for a desert storm once he left the interstate. Brody was no stranger to these sudden, fierce squalls and the very real danger they presented. He'd lived in Kingman a lifetime or two ago—and he remembered how quickly water could pool on roads not built for drainage.

They'd squelched their way up the final few yards to a small cabin barely larger than the garden shed at his Nashville estate. It had been difficult to get a clear picture as they'd climbed up the hill, but it had looked like one of those build-your-own log cabins that continued to grow as the owner saw fit. A little quirky, a whole lot individual, and right at that moment, a most welcomed sight.

He must have hesitated in some way, because the big cowboy had tucked a finger under Brody's chin. They stared at each other for several heartbeats. *"Let me help you."* The words brushed over Brody like a

23

balm, soothing his frazzled nerves and providing the last bit of reassurance he'd needed.

His savior dug in his pocket, came out with a ring of keys, and after opening the door, he ushered Brody inside.

"Sorry," he said, drawing Brody's attention. He pressed a hand to Brody's lower back and gently guided him the rest of the way through the door. The connection was like a live wire pressed against his spine—but as soon as Brody cleared the threshold, the stranger closed the door, then dropped his hand and turned away.

"I know it's not much. I, uh…I just bought the land last month. This little cabin came with, but it's definitely an as-is add on. It's not much, I know, but it should keep us dry, and we're high enough flash floods won't be a problem."

While he spoke, the cowboy hung his soggy black Stetson on a shelf nailed to the wall, before squeezing onto a very narrow bench that hugged the small space next to the front door. He tugged off his boots, then yanked his T-shirt over his head. He twisted the shirt to wring it out, then used it to wipe the mud from his boots. Water and mud pooled beneath him onto a welcome mat.

Brody swallowed hard at the six-foot-plus vision in front of him. If there had been any justice in the world, Brody would look like that, instead of the barely five-nine, buck-sixty-soaking-wet he was. He wasn't unattractive, but if he'd looked like the man in front of him, he'd be a god instead of just a megastar. He almost laughed.

Covering his moment of nervous humor, Brody asked, "What did you say your name was, again?"

"Whit. Whit Truman." He stood, his tall, lean body seeming to rise forever, the bare expanse of chest at the perfect height to give Brody ideas of tasting those tiny copper nipples. He shook himself out of the worst possible fantasy imaginable under the circumstances and cleared his throat.

"I'm...Brody Kent..." God, he'd already said that. Could things get any worse than this?

"Yeah, I know. I think we covered that." The man smiled, laugh lines fanning out from his brown eyes and deep dimples creasing both cheeks, and yeah...that was worse. *Way worse.*

Tearing his gaze away, Brody looked around the surprisingly shabby chic interior. From the remote location and rugged exterior, he'd have guessed hunt camp camouflage or even lawn chairs. An overstuffed couch and chair in bold rust and cream stripes were arranged around a wood stove. He could see straight into a small kitchen on the far side of the room. A cafe style table with two wire-back seats was in front of a large window that looked out into a solid wall of gray...the result of the heavy rainfall that was nearly deafening as it pounded on the roof.

Searching for something safe to say, Brody drew on his years of experience as a professional guest.

"You have a nice home," he offered, then realized how lame that sounded.

Whit laughed, a rich sound that bounced around inside Brody's head, competing with the rain and thunder. "I'm sure it's nothing like you're used to, however as of three weeks ago, it's mine. I lucked out and found some nice furniture at the consignment store in Kingman so I didn't have to live with the previous owner's camping gear. I might not be here every day, but I do like to be comfortable when I am. Would you mind stepping over here and taking off your wet things? I'll get you a towel, if you'll give me a sec."

With all the easy comfort of an athlete in the locker room, Whit unbuttoned the fly on his jeans then pushed his wet clothes to the floor. He stalked toward the bedroom, and Brody forced himself to look away from the tight white globes of the other man's ass.

Was he expected to strip, too? Brody blinked. Really? Stand right here and undress in front of a complete stranger? Even a sexy-as-hell cowboy? Wait...*especially* in front of a sexy-as-hell cowboy. Even shivering and soaked down to his underwear, looking at six-plus-something of naked man pressed every one of the damned buttons he needed to keep in the off position.

Karma laughed in his ear, a mocking raucous sound, giving back some of his own. Because this certainly wouldn't rank anywhere close to the first time he'd gotten naked with somebody he just met. And wasn't that part of the problem?

Brody Kent had hit the charts at twenty years old and never looked back. Taking life by storm, drinking and fucking his way through America on one concert tour after another, while earning more millions than any single person had a right to. For the first ten years, he'd taken his pleasure in the women who had thrown themselves in his direction. Men too—although from necessity, that had been much less frequent—usually confined to a one-off or a manager-with-benefits arrangement with Tim. When he'd hit the big three-oh, the thrill of waking up in a new city every morning started to lose its shiny—he got tired of asking. It was even worse having to ask the blonde or brunette de jour for her name before he thanked her and said goodbye. Eventually, he realized he was just another trophy, and the sex was as meaningless for them as it was for him. He hadn't gone looking for serious, and he'd remained perfectly happy as single. As the need to fill his life with a never-ending series of one-night stands had ebbed, he'd had his first serious girlfriend. Or at least that was how the press had framed his six-week-long fling with fellow country music star Dabney Hill—and the real start of his love-hate relationship with the media. They loved to invade every moment of his life, and he hated everything about the lack of privacy.

A noise from the bedroom shook him from his reverie. He supposed he should take off his boots, he conceded. Moving to the bench, he perched on the edge and pulled off one boot, then the other. He took the shirt Whit had used and wiped the mud from his boots before setting them on the floor to dry.

"You might as well take off your hat and shirt," Whit said, coming back into the room. Brody looked up.

"Oh, hey," Whit said at whatever expression he'd caught on Brody's face. "About that reporter…he's not going to get up here in this weather. You're safe, I promise. I'll uh…look you go in the bathroom and change—are there some dry clothes in that bag?" he nodded in the direction of the bedroom, and Brody noticed his overnight bag on the floor next to the bed.

Brody nodded, feeling tongue-tied. He wanted nothing more than to drop his clothes on the bedroom floor, throw himself onto the bed and curl up into a tight ball. Maybe sleep away the fallout from the last month of his life. His gaze dropped to the floor, and he saw the ever-expanding pool of water dripping from his clothes and hat had started leaking over the edges of the welcome mat. He unbuttoned his shirt and peeled it back from his wet skin. Standing, he put his shirt and his hat on the same peg, before turning to face Whit.

Brody was so often photographed with his hat on, people were often caught off-guard in person—but if his bald head surprised Whit, he didn't show it.

Instead, he looked politely somewhere to Brody's left and held out a towel.

"How's the knee?"

Brody blinked stupidly for a minute before he remembered he'd twisted it crossing the creek. "Fine. Just okay. Might be a little sore tomorrow, but I only wrenched it."

"Okay, good. Bathroom's back there. I'll be in the kitchen. Do you want some coffee or tea? Or maybe something stronger?"

"I wouldn't say no to something stronger," Brody said. Vowing to return to wipe up his trail of water, he opted to leave his jeans on. He slung the towel around his shoulders and walked quickly to the bathroom, stopping to grab his bag along the way. He eyed the double bed on his way past, and wondered if Whit's manners would extend to letting his guest have the bed. Or maybe they'd be out of here before nightfall. *Yeah, right.*

The bathroom was small, barely six feet wide and maybe eight feet deep. The log walls gave the room the feel of a sauna. Brody blinked at the tub…a galvanized steel horse trough, set against the back wall. With a flick of his wrist, Brody swung the bathroom door closed and started peeling off his wet jeans. He looked back almost guiltily at the door then realized he was being silly. Whit had sent him in here, and surely he wouldn't mind if Brody availed himself of the facilities.

After putting the plug in the drain, Brody turned on the water to let the tub fill. Opening his bag, he removed his shaving kit and put it on the counter next to the sink. He'd been traveling all night and not only look like a drowned rat but felt like one too. He quickly ran an electric razor over the parts of his scalp that still grew hair, brushed his teeth, then tucked everything back in the shaving kit.

His skin felt extra sensitive as he slowly submerged his legs and then hips and then his back into the large tub. Sighing with pleasure, he leaned against the tub and looked out through the window that was being pelted with rain and hail now from the outside. They were definitely here for the long haul. He needed to remember to call Cass as soon as he finished his bath. A splash of cold water hit his foot, and he quickly turned off the spigot. He must have drained the hot water heater. Damn, he hadn't left a bit for his host.

A dull thud on the door made him jump as the door swung slowly open to reveal Whit standing there with an enormous soup pot.

"Oh shit, sorry," Whit said, his face flushing. "I knocked, but the door swung open. I heard you run the water, but it's a small solar tank. I put water on the stove to heat to top it off?" He held the pot out as evidence. "Mind if I…"

"Uh…sure," Brody said, as if there was any real choice. He drew his knees up, providing a modicum of privacy, as well as making room for the hot water to be poured in.

Studiously avoiding meeting his gaze, Whit focused on his task, then walked back to the door. With his hand on the knob, he said, "Want me to put on another pot?"

"No, that's okay. It's enough for me. Unless you— Uh…no thanks."

Whit nodded and pulled the door shut. This time there was a definite snick as the door latched.

Brody was unexpectedly grinning as he scooted down in the tub and tilted his neck backward to get his head in the hot water. *Mmm, that feels good.* He reached for the bottle of woodsy-scented shampoo and massaged the liquid into his scalp, then rinsed it away. He'd come perilously close to offering to share his bath with the lanky cowboy. What was wrong with him? Was he really that foolhardy? Hadn't he had enough of fantasies and foolish dreams? He knew better, knew that the only person he should be trusting for a very long time, was himself.

Shifting in the tub as the warm water flowed over him, Brody tried to figure out how long it had been since he'd been with someone who didn't want anything from him. So far, Whit had felt like the exception to that rule. They'd known each other for less than two hours, and yet Whit had seemed to know instinctively what Brody needed, and worked hard to meet those needs without ever being asked.

He hadn't questioned why Brody had turned off the road, couldn't have known that it was the headlights from his truck that guided Brody's decision to leave the pavement. And thank God it had, because without that signal, Brody would never have realized help was within reach. He and the reporter would've continued careening down that road until there'd been an accident. So, in many ways, Whit had saved him.

Closing his eyes, he forced himself to unclench his jaw along with the muscles in his arms and legs. As he relaxed deeper into the warm tub, Brody ran a hand down his chest and sucked in a breath at the pleasurable sensations that shot through him. He hadn't conjured up sexy fantasies in a long time.

Drawing on long buried memories, he drifted back to a scene where he was in a man's arms and his head was bent down over the other man's cock. His breath quickened as he slid his fingers along his shaft in time with the memory of his mouth on another man's dick. In his fantasy, he looked up into the face of his lover, unsurprised to find Whit smiling down at him, his dimples flashing wickedly. Brody's hand moved faster.

From the moment the man had suggested they start over with hello, Brody had been lost. He'd been caught in the deep brown gaze, the lines that fanned away from his eyes, the barely-there beard. Sexy as sin.

Rocking his hips up and down as he got closer, Brody closed his lids, keeping Whit's face in his head. He didn't even bother to stop himself from fantasizing about what the cowboy's kiss would taste like, about how it would feel to have those large calloused hands stroking his cock instead of his own. With Whit's name on his lips, his entire body tightened down before exploding into a thousand delicious pieces, his hips bucking, ropes of cum spurting over his fingers and across his chest.

Chapter Three

Holy hell—Whit leaned hard against the countertop, nearly to the point of pain…anything to keep from shooting a load in his jeans while he stood in his kitchen, ostensibly minding his own business. He'd been trying hard to un-see the very naked Brody Kent—who'd so casually allowed him to pour hot water into the tub—and failing miserably. But that was before the rhythmic sound of water slapping carried through the shared wall between the bathroom and the kitchen.

Whit had lived in the WSR bunkhouses off and on for nearly ten years. Each of the dorms held one main room with a kitchen and television area plus four private bedrooms. Private had always been a relative term, depending on how many men the bunkhouse held at a time. There were times when the sound of a man jerking one off in the shower or a couple of men fucking carried in the stillness of a desert night. Sometimes he'd been the one making the noises, other times he was the one to turn up the television, offering a modicum of privacy. All of the men at the WSR knew there was a chance they'd be heard if they stayed in an occupied dorm—and they all knew where they could go for more privacy.

Did Brody realize Whit could hear him as he pleasured himself in the bathtub? The honorable thing to do would be to walk outside, drench his head in more of the cold rain, soak through another pair of jeans, maybe even stick his head in the ice chest. But he hadn't been able to help himself, he'd stayed standing stock-still, making no noise, imagining every stroke on that slick wet skin with his hand on Brody's cock.

Whit's knees went a little weak, and he grabbed the edge of the counter for support. Looking down, he realized his hands were actually shaking and he was so hard there was little doubt his zipper was going to leave marks on the underside of his cock. Reaching inside his jeans to adjust himself, he moaned at the contact, then bit back a curse.

Some small voice told Whit to calm down. Brody had called Cass, looking for respite from the publicity nightmare swirling around him. Whit couldn't begin to fathom what it would be like to live your life in a fishbowl, to have others see you as nothing more than a commodity. The reporter following him today could have caused serious harm, and all for what? To "expose" where the man went on vacation? To tell the world who Brody slept with? *Oh hell no.*

Whit hadn't thought much about it when he'd stepped from his wet clothes in the front room, but he was sure he hadn't imagined the interest that flared in Brody's eyes. But interest didn't necessarily lead to action. Something about Brody was different from anyone Whit had ever known. *Always has been.*

Despite the fact Whit wanted Brody Kent more than he'd ever wanted any other man, he could honestly say he didn't want to join a long line of faceless fucks. His friend Park liked to point out that fate seemed to put people in the path of those they needed to meet—it was an interesting idea. Brody might think today had been one long series of mishaps after another—missing the turnoff, the reporter, the near accident in the torrential rain.

From Whit's perspective, he was now destined to spend at least one, but possibly two or three or four days in an isolated cabin with a man he'd been sure he'd dislike. Between a childhood memory and the spate of negative publicity, Whit had been certain Brody was an arrogant ass, at best—or more likely, a closet case who'd married just to save his career. That hadn't been the case so far. Instead, every time he looked at Brody, he saw a man with haunted eyes and a story to tell. A man he wanted to hold until he felt safe. And wasn't that a kick in the ass?

Whit turned on the water to fill the soup pot once again. Only this time, he decided to actually make some soup. Not normally a summertime meal, because it was just too damned hot, it would go good after their chill. Plus, he had a chicken in the small freezer. He kept the water running to thaw the wrapping enough so he could put the chicken in the pot. He didn't hear Brody enter the room, but the hair on the nape of his neck rose with awareness.

"Why are you doing this?" Brody's voice was serious, and Whit took a quick glance over his shoulder to confirm his expression matched the tone. He nearly lost his breath at the sight of Brody, dressed in faded blue jeans and a white T-shirt. Simple and perfect.

"If the question is why am I making soup, it's because I don't have too many food options here and a pot of hot soup seemed like a good idea on a day like this." He used his chin to point toward the window as he peeled off the plastic wrap and dropped the chicken into the pot.

Brody snorted. He could tell the man wanted to laugh, but he was determined to make his point.

"Thank you. For everything you did to get rid of that reporter and to drag me up the hill. I wouldn't have made it without you."

His chest squeezed at Brody's heartfelt words. "You're welcome. And I suspect you'd have been just fine, but I'm glad I was there to help. I can't imagine what it must be like to have complete strangers trying to track your every move."

"I'd really hoped for a few days away from everything. That's why I called Cass; he's always been a friend I could count on when I needed to get in touch with reality."

Whit smiled. "Cass is pretty good at telling it like it is. Have you known him long?" Whit rummaged through the refrigerator and came up with some celery, carrots, and an onion. Chopping the vegetables, Whit gave Brody a quick glance, but he seemed lost in thought. After a minute, he added the seasonings and the rest of the ingredients to his stockpot. Then finally turned to face Brody, to find the man watching him, his light eyes intense, a small smile playing about his mouth. Whit stared. What would it be like to have that smile focused on him, and not a memory of another man?

Brody shook himself, a little shudder that made Whit want to moan. Finally, he began. "Cass sponsored a charity event I worked on when I was first getting started. One of the true legends of country music was the headliner, and he wasn't too thrilled with having some young punk—that's what he called me—on the publicity posters along with him. Said it wasn't respectful." Brody paused in his story as Whit opened a cabinet and brought out two rocks glasses and set them on the counter.

"Sorry, didn't mean to interrupt. I've got Jim Beam or Corona."

"How long until the soup is ready—you did say soup, right?"

Whit laughed. "Yeah, it's soup, but it won't be ready for a couple of hours. Are you hungry?"

"Nope, not yet. I'd'a picked beer if we were eating, but yeah...JB will go down nice right now. It's been a helluva day." Whit poured while Brody resumed his story.

"Anyway like all young bucks, I was pretty damn full of myself. I thought the old fool needed to get out of my way. Country music was changing—the old guard needed to get with the times. People didn't want to sit and listen to some old song about a man who dies of a broken heart or some woman standing by her man.

"I was…twenty-one? Twenty-two? My first album—*Making Memories*—had gone platinum, and I believed I could do no wrong. I had about half a dozen hangers-on, including my manager—Tim Fichter—all telling me I was right. My name and face needed to be right there on all the publicity, my star was shining and the old man's was fading. Yada-yada." He took two good swallows of his drink, then set the glass on the counter. Whit refilled it without being asked.

"Anyway, I'd gotten myself all worked up." Brody smiled at the memory. "You might have noticed Cass is a bit bigger than I am. In fact"—he eyed Whit, a slow perusal from head to toes that had things standing up and taking notice—"you remind me a bit of the big cowboy. Where was I? Oh yeah—Cass muscled me outside. Just up and hauled me outta there by the scruff of my neck. He chewed my ass. Reminded me that my career was thanks to those who done the hard work before me. Said I should never forget where I came from—and that included every man or woman who'd ever sang at the Grand Ole Opry."

Brody finished of his drink while Whit sipped his more slowly then topped them off once again. They were still standing in the small kitchen, but he didn't want to break the spell, so he just waited for Brody to continue.

"It was a damned fine ass-chewing—and well-deserved, I might add. Afterward, we went out and got shit-faced together, but I didn't forget the lesson. The next day, I was contrite and made some concessions that had Tim screaming about market and exposure, and kinds of other shit I didn't want to hear.

"But you know…Cass was right. The man had earned his place at top-billing, had earned it playing every honkytonk that would have him, while country music was just starting to find a foothold—way before it went mainstream. I needed to pay him his due with my respect." He took another sip, then set his glass on the counter with a thunk.

"The funny thing is…after that, the old man took me under his wing…taught me shit about music, introduced me to some important people who made a difference in my career. I'd'a missed that without Cass's intervention. It taught me an important lesson. No matter how big you are, there's always somebody who was big before you, and there's always somebody who's gonna be bigger than you crawling up your ass on the charts." He paused, shifting his gaze to the windows before letting out a long sigh.

"It also taught me the importance of knowing at least one person who will tell you what you need to hear—not what you want to hear."

God, Whit wanted to be that person. Brody was the first man he'd ever loved—even if he'd been too young at the time to know what that meant. All his life, Brody Kent represented the unobtainable—Whit had used his fantasies of Brody to avoid any chance of commitment in his real life. He'd safely adored Brody from afar. Now faced with the reality of the man, he thought maybe this was more like love at first sight—an insta-wham of blinding clarity with the real man, and not just the memory or the fantasy. He hadn't realized that today was going to change his life forever. But it just had.

And, amazingly—shockingly—he wasn't the least bit interested in fighting the changes. Instead, here he was, gearing up for a different fight altogether. The fight for Brody Kent's heart.

Chapter Four

Brody woke up warm and well-rested, and more than a little surprised to discover he'd fallen asleep on the comfortable living room sofa. There was a pillow under his head, and a fleece throw over his shoulders, neither of which he remembered being there previously. Oh how he'd dreamed of afternoons like this—time to laze about, sleep if he wanted, or do—well, whatever it was regular folks did. People without a million screaming demands, people who weren't surrounded 24/7 by managers and producers and reporters and…leeches.

Being out here with the knowledge that he was completely cut off from that part of his life—at least until the weather cleared and the creek calmed—was liberating. He didn't have to be 'on' all the time, ready for the next fan moment.

Chewing on that thought for a minute, Brody had to laugh at himself. Because as much as he railed against the trappings of his career, he had to admit he wanted Whit to know—and to love—his music. Just how crazy did that make him?

The internal laughter died at that thought. What *was* wrong with him? Nothing made him happy anymore. He'd had great hopes with Lisa. At least at first. Six months ago he'd thought he might be nearing some kind of a breakdown. He'd become jaded, the music he tried to write was stale, and he'd refused to sign a new contract with the record company. He'd seriously been considering retirement. Noticing his discontent, Tim had encouraged him to get away awhile and booked a vacation for him at Punta de Mita in Mexico. He'd stayed holed up in his suite at the Four Seasons for nearly a week before he ventured out to the beach. The beautiful blonde Lisa Bennington and a small group of her friends were playing a wild game of volleyball, and Brody fell right into the group. The rest, as they say, was history. Their whirlwind romance played out in front of the press and Brody found himself one half of America's latest sweethearts. They'd married last month, and three days later, they were in their respective attorneys offices, filing for an annulment.

Lisa was beautiful, sweet, funny, athletic...all the things he found attractive—and yet he hadn't loved her. Apparently the feeling was mutual. And now...because of the premarital agreements and the grounds used to file for the annulment, rumors were spreading that he was gay.

For the last three weeks, no matter what lengths he went to for privacy, someone from the press always showed up—until he'd had to face the fact that someone in his inner circle had to be selling him out. Or Lisa had paid for a very good private investigator.

Either way, he no longer knew whom he could trust—no longer had the luxury of pretending everything was okay. Not by a long shot.

Which was why he'd turned to Cass. Once he got to the WSR, he could count on the total discretion of his old friend. And yet even way out here—a reporter had found him.

Maybe the best thing to do would be to avoid everyone, completely. To find someplace like this to call his own for a year—or ten—and let all the furor fade away. What would that be like? To start over—to build his own place, on his own land?

Brody pushed upright, energized by the thought. He sat for a long moment, breathing in the rich aroma of the homemade chicken soup, enjoying the homey feel of the small cabin, the idea of new beginnings. Glancing around the room, he saw his guitar case propped against the wall, wiped clean of the rain and mud spatter that marred the surface earlier. God, he must really have been out of it, if he hadn't checked his baby yet. Whit must have cleaned it for him.

His fingers itched to touch the strings, a chord already echoing in his head. Did he dare try? It had been so long since the words had come…had pushed at him like this.

Irresistibly drawn, he opened the case as soon as he brought it to the couch. He stared for a long moment before taking out his spiral notepad and pencil and placing them on the table. He spent a minute running trembling fingers over her sleek lines before lovingly removing the guitar. He owned dozens of guitars he supposed, but this—his Les Paul Gibson—was his favorite. His baby. They used to make beautiful music together, back when the words still came.

From where he sat, he could see both the bedroom and the kitchen were empty…he played a riff. Fingered the frets, plucked out a few notes, adjusted the tuning keys. The chord was still in his head. He played it and another followed. Then another.

Brody narrowed his eyes and played the combination again. And again. He stilled his fingers and hummed, adding a few more notes. Reaching for his pencil, he jotted down the notes. His fingers still shaking slightly as he added a title. Without giving himself time to think…or worry…he wrote the first words that came to mind, a private brainstorming session. Not lyrics—not yet. Just a jumble of words to evoke the feelings this song would convey.

Home. Relief. Safety. Destiny. Starting over. Freedom. Words spilled out, a dam bursting, crumbling under the wave of emotions. Finally, he pushed the notebook away and went back to the music. With his eyes closed, he played the opening a few times, then let his fingers wander. This was how the magic worked for him, patterns emerged, notes and words sometimes fused. Sometimes not.

Humming along, occasionally whispering a word or phrase, the song seemingly wrote itself, leaving Brody feeling as if he were trying to keep up. Finally, he opened his eyes—to find his inspiration staring right back at him.

Whit leaned in the doorway to the kitchen, his thumbs hooked in the pockets of his faded jeans, navy blue T-shirt loose and comfortable-looking, one bare foot crossed over the other. They stared at each other for a long moment—and he would swear the temperature rose at least ten degrees in the space that separated them. Whit's brown eyes blazed with enough heat to set off the smoke alarm, and there was no mistaking that bulge just west of center for anything other than arousal. A fantasy wormed into his brain. Whit would cross the room and jerk him to his feet, drag him off to the bedroom, and fuck his brains out. Something of his thoughts must have shown, because Whit sucked in a sharp breath, his nostrils flared, and those damn eyes darkened even more.

Brody cleared his throat. "Sorry. I didn't think you were here. I didn't mean to disturb—"

"Dinner's ready," Whit interrupted, his voice husky with unexpressed desire. He turned back toward the kitchen, leaving Brody nodding to an empty room.

Phew.

Needing a few moments to pull himself together, Brody put his guitar in the case, then scribbled a few more notes. In the distant past, he'd have hustled the man off to his bed for an afternoon of uncomplicated sex, but early in his career, Tim had made him see the necessity of hiding his bisexual nature. Maybe it was the prolonged steady diet of female companions that heightened his appetite for Whit. Whatever the reason, logic said this was a time to lay low—because if evidence of even a single embrace from another man came to light...his career would be over. One thing he'd finally gotten through his hard head—there wasn't anyone he should trust. Not even the sexy cowboy who'd ridden to his rescue. When he finally had his lust under control, he strolled to the kitchen.

Chapter Five

After their earlier drinks, Brody had fallen asleep mid-comment, nearly as soon as they'd shifted to sit in the living room. Whit couldn't blame him. He'd traveled through the night, had a near miss with the reporter, then had to hike a mile through the mud and rain. The poor man had to be exhausted. Resisting the urge to brush a hand along Brody's back and join him on the couch, Whit had put a pillow under his head and covered him with a light blanket. Then he'd moved to sit on the screened-in porch, just staring at the rain and thinking about life. And Brody Kent.

Funny how just yesterday, he'd rolled his eyes at the spectacle surrounding Brody's brief marriage and annulment. Today, he'd not only inserted himself between Brody and a reporter, he was contemplating how to keep himself there.

Brody sauntered into the room just as Whit ladled the soup into bowls. "I'm sorry this isn't fancy. I didn't have much in the way of fresh food in the house. I took out a couple of sourdough rolls from the freezer, but I don't have a salad."

Brody walked to the sink and washed his hands before coming to the table. "The soup smells delicious, and I'm in no position to complain about the menu. Thanks for letting me sleep this afternoon. I must've really needed it."

Whit grinned. "You were in the middle of asking me a question when you stopped talking. I looked over to see why and you'd conked."

Brody laughed. "What in the world was I asking?"

Whit picked up a spoon and blew on his soup before answering. "You asked me how long I thought you might be stuck here."

"Ouch. I don't think I meant that the way it sounds." He tasted the soup. "Wow. This is delicious. Do you do a lot of cooking? Because I have to be honest, if I was told I had to make chicken soup, it would be out of a red and white can."

"I cook a little. The bunkhouses at the WSR have small kitchens in case we don't want to eat at the main house. Did you ever meet Tyler Hardin? Cass's partner?"

Brody shook his head, but kept eating, his gaze flicking back and forth between his bowl and Whit.

"Ty was a cook in the Navy before he became a SEAL. There isn't much need to do your own cooking out there if you don't want to."

"It's a little hard to picture Cass settled down. He was a bit of a player back in the day."

"Did you ever—" Whit shook his head. "Forget I even started that question. It's wrong on every level. Look, Brody, to answer your earlier question, we're going to be here another day most likely before the ground dries enough to get the truck out. It'll probably be three or four days before your car is drivable, but I'll come back and get it for you. I just want you to know…you're safe while you're here. I called Cass after you fell asleep, to let him know what happened—but you should still check in with him. He'll vouch for me, and that will make you feel better. You can just relax, let me take care of everything. I promise, no reporters are going to find you here."

Wincing inwardly at the little growl that crawled into his voice, Whit looked for a safer subject. "Want to start over again?"

Brody barked a little laugh and Whit grinned in response.

"I think we might have done that once already," Brody said. "But, I'm game if you are. How long have you worked for Cass?"

They went back and forth exchanging small pieces of themselves while sharing their meal. Brody's shoulders were no longer hunched, and he laughed easily as they discussed food and movies, books and heat versus humidity. Silly, inconsequential, safe. When Whit pushed away from the table and began to clear, Brody jumped up to help.

Brody filled the sink with water and a squirt of dish soap, while Whit finished clearing the table. Whit put his hand on Brody's back as he reached around him for the washcloth. Heat flowed up his arm at the contact, a charge of electricity that nearly rooted him to the spot. Brody smiled, hands in the soapy water and kept working, so Whit did the same.

When he returned the dishrag, Whit leaned over Brody's back, their bodies brushing against each other for the briefest of moments. Brody's quick breath at the contact matched his own. Whit waited, willing Brody to acknowledge the attraction that teased between them all evening. He'd have waited longer, if necessary, but he'd known it was coming. There was too much in the looks they'd shared, too many lingering smiles.

Brody turned off the water and rested his hands on the edge of the sink, staring down into the mass of bubbles. After a minute, he sighed, then leaned back, closing the distance between them. When he finally looked up over his shoulder, his smile slid away as he met Whit's gaze.

"Oh yeah, that's better," Whit breathed.

"I can't—" Brody said on a half moan.

Whit smiled slowly. "I think you can."

Trapping Brody against the sink, Whit ran his hand up the smaller man's arm, until he reached his face. He traced his fingers over the strong chin, the sharp cheekbones, then over the smooth scalp. When Brody didn't pull back, Whit lowered his mouth. "You're safe with me," he whispered, then brushed his lips in a gentle kiss.

Kissing Brody had his heart pounding and his cock demanding attention, but Whit kept his hips a discreet distance from temptation and the kiss light and easy.

A shiver coursed through Brody, driving his ass against Whit, and he moaned at the contact. He deepened the kiss, and Brody opened, let him in.

Whit held Brody captive while he tasted his kisses. Somewhere in the back of his head he started to wonder if he was hurting Brody the way he held him trapped against the counter, but their tongues slid together, Brody moaned for him, and Whit leaned farther into the kiss. Drawing back slightly, he gently sucked Brody's lower lip between his teeth for a soft nip. And then their tongues were back at it until Brody did the same, nipping, licking, biting. It was Whit's turn to moan.

"Brody."

His chiseled lips parted slightly at the sound of his name. For the first time, Brody wasn't trying to hide his desire. "It's inevitable, isn't it?" Brody asked him in a soft voice that reverberated all the way through Whit.

Hell yes, it was. But Whit couldn't put words in Brody's mouth. Not now when every word, every look, every touch felt so damned important.

"What's inevitable, Brody? What do you want to happen here?" His words were raw, and he couldn't hide his desire.

*

When Brody didn't answer, just ground his ass back against Whit's hard length, the big man shifted his hand on the back of his head, tilting him farther, changing the angle of their kiss. Brody's body was screaming yes…yes…yes! But there was a small corner of his mind trying to be heard over all the thundering of his heart. This was wrong, too much was at stake. He didn't know this man…

His body stiffened—and not in a good way.

Whit noticed and pulled his hips back. He gentled his kiss, licking and brushing over Brody's lips. Then the hands and the kiss were gone, opening a pool of loss and confusion in Brody's heart.

Whit stepped back, a sad smile touching his kiss-swollen lips. "Come on, let's finish up these dishes." His voice was husky, but he turned away and finished putting the food in the refrigerator.

For the first time since forever, Brody was unsure of what to do. He wanted Whit, that wasn't the question. Even if his mind couldn't sort through the complications in his life right now, his body was screaming at him to get with the program. Save a horse…all that shit.

Whit wanted him. The desire wasn't feigned, and it didn't seem to be associated with any type of fan-fuck-me syndrome. In fact—

"Have you ever listened to my music?" The words came out as an accusation, and Brody wished them back.

Without missing a beat, Whit put the salt and pepper shakers in the cabinet and named three of his biggest sellers: "Rodeo," "Rock Me Through the Night," "Party Cowboys."

Brody wanted to beat his head against the wall. One minute he's sick and tired of being a public figure—the next he's grilling a wannabe bed partner to see if he's fan enough?

Whit grabbed a dishtowel and gave him a little hip bump. "You can make a bath in the tub if you want to play in bubbles, but maybe you could finish those dishes first?" The laughter in his voice made Brody smile.

Nodding, Brody rinsed the bowl he'd been washing for several minutes and handed it to Whit. "Sorry," he said. Then thinking Whit might not realize why he was apologizing, he continued talking while he finished the dishes.

"I've spent weeks wishing somebody knew me for who I really am, not just as a—"

"Celebrity?" Whit finished for him.

"Yeah," Brody agreed. He sighed as he put the last of the dishes into the strainer and emptied the sink. "It's why I was coming to the WSR. Now here you are, treating me the way I claim I want—like nobody special—and I'm complaining."

Whit grabbed his shoulder and tugged gently, turning him. He tucked a finger under Brody's chin, but waited to speak until their gazes met. Brody fell into those damn dark eyes, his pulse setting a new rhythm that had him wanting to reach for his guitar.

"I know who you are," Whit said quietly, then named three more songs. "'Summer Days.' 'Lost Treasures.' 'Over You.'" Songs Brody had not only performed, but had written.

His breath caught, and he searched Whit's face, trying to see what was behind that calm exterior. How could he have guessed at those three deeply personal songs. Only one had been a commercial success, but they'd all been important because they'd been about his life. He'd never told that to anyone.

"Those—those are just songs," he stammered. Who was this man? Could this be an elaborate setup? Had he been herded by the Jeep to make him turn off here? As soon as the thought entered his mind, Brody tried to dismiss it. Given the weather and the circumstances, it had to be a coincidence. *Had to.*

"If you say so," Whit agreed easily. He brushed his thumb over Brody's cheek. "I would never want to pressure you to do something you don't want to do, Brody. There are too many people in your life already who are trying to use you. I don't need a thing—I don't *want* a thing. Except you. Now why don't you go to bed and I'll see you in the morning."

As the big man leaned in, Brody's lips seemed to part on their own, but Whit pressed his kiss to Brody's forehead. Without another word, Whit went to the front door, slid his feet into a pair of hiking boots, strapped on his holster, then shrugged into a dark weatherproof jacket. He mashed a cowboy hat on his head, then stepped out into the night.

Chapter Six

Brody woke the next morning surprised he'd not only slept, but slept well. He stretched on sheets that were considerably less smooth than his own thousand thread count, plumped the lumpy foam pillow, and stared up at the exposed wood beam ceiling. This was a life he'd not known since he was a kid. Simple, unadorned, practical. Making do with what you could afford instead of buying everything you wanted on a whim.

This felt…good. Working on becoming his own person these past few weeks since the annulment had been liberating—even if it had been a constant struggle to find moments of privacy—but maybe he'd been looking in the wrong places. Hadn't that been what drove him to the WSR? Even now the urgency to start running again tried to steal through him, but for the moment he was too darned relaxed to do more than stretch out his back. His muscles were tight from the hike in the mud and rain. It was a type of sore you obtained through hard work, not forty-five minutes in a private gym three days a week. The well-worked muscles felt good, too.

Brody had crawled naked between the sheets the previous night, but in the bright light of the morning that was now streaming in through the sheer curtains at the window, he remembered how Whit had kissed him. And maybe he'd fantasized—in Technicolor detail—about the bigger man joining him in bed during the night. Relieving Brody of the need to make a decision, by taking matters into his own hands. It hadn't happened, but then again, Brody had been fast asleep long before Whit returned to the cabin.

The kissing, the white-hot desire that burned between them left Brody twitchy in his skin. He wanted Whit. There was no doubt they'd be good together, but he'd made an important promise to himself...and it would hardly do to fall back into the same bad pattern of one-night stands. It would be even worse to feed into the gay rumors while the whole mess with Lisa still had all the closure of a recently-launched nuclear weapon.

Since there was no noise from the other room, he assumed Whit was still asleep on the couch. Dancing away from the devil who tempted him to take the cowboy for a ride, Brody kicked back the covers and slipped back into his jeans. He pulled a clean T-shirt from his bag, then shuffled into the bathroom. Once he was shaved and minty fresh, he felt ready to face Whit and whatever challenges the day might bring.

The empty living room surprised him. There was no sign the other man slept on the couch, and a quick glance toward the other room confirmed the cabin was empty. The smell of coffee drew him into the kitchen. Half a pot waited, along with a mug and a note. Brody filled his cup, his gaze drifting back toward the living room to where his guitar still leaned against the wall. His fingers itched. In a good way. Huh…in a good way. *In a Good Way*. The words started chasing themselves, getting tangled in notes and chords.

Brody sipped his coffee, letting the words play a little longer, part of him marveling at the rediscovery of his music. He couldn't remember how many years it had been since there were two songs fighting for his attention.

Finally, the noise in his head became too loud. He needed to give it voice. He refilled his mug, then fingered the note before pulling it closer to read.

Brody,

Good morning. I hope you slept well—sorry about any lumps in the bed. Feel free to rummage around for breakfast. I'm afraid there's not much—I wasn't expecting company. :)

I am out working on freeing up my truck. If I'm not back by lunchtime, help yourself to more soup.

Back soon,

Whit

P.S. There's OJ in the fridge, but no milk—sorry.

Since he rarely ate breakfast anyway, the limited menu wasn't a problem. Brody ran his fingers over the note, a smile playing about his mouth as he realized what he was doing. He was a romantic at heart—and even though he had no intention of allowing this little dance between him and Whit to continue—it was nice to be desired. In a good way. *In a Good Way.*

Bringing his mug with him, Brody went to get his guitar. "Honey, I'm home."

*

"Cass? It's me, Whit."

Laughter barked out at him. "Yes, I know. I do have caller ID. How's the damage from the storm?"

"Nothing major. I just finished walking most of the land and only saw a few downed branches. The cabin held up just fine. How are things at the WSR?"

"Nothing major here, either. The horses were excited during the worst of the thunder and lightning, but Drew and Jesse took care of things. How's your truck? Are you going to be able to get it out today?"

"I'm working on it right now. It's not as bad as I thought, although, I put a damn dent in the driver side door. That just pisses me off. Oh well, nothing I can do about it now. I'll take it to Kingman next time Ty needs to go to town. Anyway, the reason I called...I'm probably going to be able to get my truck out in a couple of hours. I'll bring Brody, but his car isn't going anywhere. I didn't realize it at the time, but he busted an axle when he came up over the drainage ditch."

"No problem. We'll get one of the trucks with a winch on it to get it out of the mud after a couple of days. Then he can call the rental company. He said he was planning on staying a while anyway, so being without a car for a few days shouldn't be a problem. How are things going between you two? I got the impression—"

"Hang on, Cass. Someone's coming." The only sound that should have been out here was the wind through the trees and birdsong. The approaching vehicle was loud, an engine pushing fast.

"Brody?" Cass asked after a minute, but there was tension in his voice.

"It's a vehicle. *Fuck*. It's the goddamn reporter who was here yesterday. Brody's up at the cabin—out of sight. Other than his car still stuck in the mud, there's no sign of him. Stay on the line."

Whit set his phone on the hood of his truck, shifted his shovel to his other hand, and rested his right hand on the butt of his forty-five.

Without actually pulling off the main road and onto Whit's land, the Jeep came to a stop, and the reporter climbed out. In his late thirties or early forties, the man had shaggy long black hair and wore thick horn-rimmed glasses. His mud-splattered jeans suggested he was wearing the same clothes as yesterday. There hadn't been even a single stray footprint on the other side of the creek. So he knew the reporter would be on a fishing trip—as long as

Brody stayed up top there was nothing to give him away.

"Forget something?" Whit asked.

"I came back to find Brody Kent. He around?"

"If that's the guy who belongs to the white car, he's gonna need to come back and get it towed outta here. The axle broke clean in two."

The man got down on his haunches and studied the underside of the white car. He stood, brushed off the knees of his jeans, and looked around as if he expected to see Brody just standing there somewhere. "If his car's here, then he's here."

"No, dumb shit. Someone in a big black Hummer about the size of a tank picked him up about an hour after you ran him off the road. You're a reporter right? What did you say yesterday? TYZ?"

"Yeah," the man said. "Would you be interested in giving me an exclusive? I've got another camera in the Jeep." He smiled like they were old friends and took a step closer. "You can give me back my other camera and tell me what you and Brody talked about. Maybe describe the Hummer and—"

"And when the guy you were chasing comes back for this piece of shit car," Whit interrupted, "I'm gonna suggest he contact your insurance company. I don't mind being an eyewitness to report how you ran him off the road. When you meet up again, you can ask him for the camera, because he took it when he left. You got any other stupid questions?"

"How do I know he's not staying here with you?"

Whit nodded, grateful he'd untied the rope that they'd used to help them across the creek yesterday. Unless the reporter was a master tracker, there wasn't any evidence of a crossing underneath all the leaves and other debris left behind from the flash flood. "Yep, another stupid question. You can see inside my truck. Does it look like I have a guest?"

"Are you telling me you stayed out here all night?"

"Are you telling me you have a brain? I'll try to use short words. The man who was driving that car isn't here. A vehicle picked him up roughly an hour after you ran him off the road. The Hummer came from that way—it went back that way." He pointed south. "I suppose they could have circled back around, but since the car was headed south to begin with, that's probably the way they went. Now unless you're here to get that car"—he pointed with his chin, and put his hand back on the butt of his gun—"I suggest you get the fuck outta here and let me get back to digging my way out. I need to get home." Whit started to turn away, hoping the reporter would take the action for the dismissal it was.

"Mind giving me your name and address?" the reporter ventured. Ballsy bastard.

Whit gave him a long look, then dropped the shovel and reached for his phone. He made a show of swiping the screen and pointing the device at the reporter. "You want to smile for your photo?" he asked, pushing the button and wondering if he'd just hung up on Cass. The click of the camera app was nice and loud. Whit turned the camera on the Jeep and then toward the white car. The reporter started backing away, slowly at first, then more quickly as Whit got closer.

"Don't worry about getting my name and home address right now. I'm sure the insurance company will be contacting you soon enough. Hell, maybe I should even call the police, since you were clearly attempting to harm the driver of the other car when you deliberately forced him off the road. Yeah, my memory is getting better with each passing minute. Good thing I got these photos…" Whit kept talking as the reporter climbed in his Jeep, started the engine, then roared off, continuing south along the county road.

Cass was laughing when, with a few muttered curse words. Whit finally figured out how to close the camera and resume his call. "Did you hear most of that?" he asked.

"Yeah, I got it. You did good, Whit. Listen, I know you didn't seem to be overly happy about Brody Kent staying here at the ranch when I invited him—I should have asked. Is there some history I should know about?"

Whit thought about the way the question was phrased and figured he could answer it honestly enough. "No."

There was a pause. "Is there a history you think I *shouldn't* know about?" Cass amended.

Shit. "Not really. I knew him a long time ago. He doesn't even remember me."

"Oh—uh. Well hell. I'm sorry, Whit. I'm sure he didn't mean—uh—Brody was kinda wild when he was younger."

When Whit realized Cass assumed he was talking about sex, he rushed to reassure him. "Nothing like that, boss. I knew him in school. He was older than me—no reason to remember is all I meant. I've got the truck just about out, maybe another hour, then I'll go get Brody from the cabin and bring him to the WSR."

"Damn…either you're trying to change the subject or you're a bit focused. Are you sure everything is okay between the two of you…shit. Was there any problem last night? Did you—"

"No, dammit. We'll be there soon, Cass." He ended the call before his too-perceptive boss could ask anything further. Cass was turning into as big a matchmaker as Ty. Couple of old busybodies.

Chapter Seven

"No, Cass, nothing's wrong." Brody had already answered the question once. The first time had been right after they'd arrived, and Whit excused himself to go to the barn to check on his horse. Brody had stood there next to the truck, watching as Whit's long legs carried him across the dirt yard. He'd turned to find Cass staring at him. He'd reassured his host that nothing was the matter, then reached into the backseat of the truck to get a suitcase. With Cass's help, they'd made it in two trips, putting everything in the bigger of the two bedrooms. Brody was feeling…bruised. Twitchy in his skin again. Even though the ranch was miles off the main road, and the only people here were Cass's employees and friends, it felt far more public than the little cabin at the top of the hill. He'd been staring at the pile of suitcases when Cass had asked again if he was all right.

Trying to deflect the attention, Brody played the role of good guest. "This guest house is great, Cass. There're so many more buildings than when I was here last."

"More buildings, more men. It's been close to seven years since the last time you stayed."

"Bullshit! No way it's been that long."

Cass nodded. "Yep. We've got three of these casitas and are planning several more. Two bunkhouses." He frowned. "We were in the process of building another, but we had some trouble. It's a long story I can tell you over drinks later, if you like." Cass looked at all the bags and started to laugh. "Goddamn, Brody. When you said you wanted to stay a while, I didn't realize you wanted to move in. One...two...three..." He laughed harder. "I understand the guitars, but seven suitcases?"

Brody laughed at Cass's exaggeration, then realized he was right. There were seven bags. "Shit, Cass. We brought Whit's stuff inside, too." He grabbed the handle of the big olive green canvas bag. "You get that one—we can put it back in his truck." He pointed at the matching bag on the floor.

"I got it, but we're going to take it into the second bedroom. I know you want your space, but I think it's best if you have someone around as a makeshift bodyguard."

"Oh hell no. I can't ask Whit to do that, and I can't ask you to give up one of your ranch hands. Tell me, Cass—truth here—is my staying going to present a problem for you?"

"Not in the least. This casita was vacant, and as far as I'm concerned, you can have it as long as you want. But for the next week and a half, we are going to have people on the ranch who don't live here. I told you a little bit about it on the phone. We're setting up for a special event, twenty kids and teens who are sick get to experience ranch life for a day. We are treating it like a festival. We're having a couple of tents set up, a petting zoo, even a pony ride. It will be over by next Sunday, but until then, I'm having Whit stick close to you. I didn't like the sound of that reporter. He was tenacious as hell."

Brody followed Cass into the other bedroom where they left Whit's bags then to the kitchen. "The reporter was an ass," he agreed. "But he took off quick enough once Whit pulled his gun. I don't think he's likely to come back."

Cass frowned. "He did come back. This morning. Didn't Whit tell you? I was on the phone and heard the whole thing. Whit convinced him you had gotten a ride and headed south right after the accident. That's exactly my point. You need someone who can run interference, if necessary."

Brody stared at Cass, unable to think of what to say. The reporter had come back looking for him?

Cass opened the refrigerator. "Want a beer?" he asked. Without waiting for an answer, he removed two bottles of Corona and a lime.

"Yeah. Please. What did Whit do?"

Cass searched the drawers for a knife, sliced the lime, then opened the bottles. He put a slice in the neck of each and handed one to Brody. "Ty stocked the place for you. Plenty of food and drink. I wasn't sure if you'd want to take meals at the main house or not. Tyler fixes enough food for everyone on-site, but that also means a loss of your privacy, since all the men eat with us. You don't need to decide now—there's always plenty. My men all know you're here, no getting around that, I'm afraid, but I trust each one of them with my life, Brody. We've had a long year—part of that story we'll talk about over drinks one night. You want to ride one of the horses, tell Whit, he'll fix you up."

Brody squeezed the tart fruit, pushing it rind and all, into his beer, then took a long swallow. "And Whit did what?" he asked again.

With a sigh, Cass relayed the entire conversation. When he was finished, he added, "I heard the whole thing. It's why I want him by your side. The reporter isn't likely to be deterred, and it won't take much digging to find a connection between the two of us. Are you really sure being here is the best choice?"

Brody blew out a breath, knowing he was tempting fate by staying here now that a reporter tracked him to the area, but unable to force himself to leave. "I'll risk it, if you're sure you don't mind. But there's no need to tie Whit down because of my choice."

"I know he's a little young, and hard on the eyes, but give the guy a break, Kent."

"Hah, very funny. You know damned well—" Brody bit his lip to keep from saying more.

"Yeah, I do. I know you, Brody. You finally got tired of fucking around and you thought Lisa Bennington was going to be enough to hold your attention."

"Think I was wrong to try?" Brody asked. "You settled down. You think this Tyler is Mr. Right for you?"

"No," Cass drew the word out. "I don't think you're wrong. You know me, too, Brody. We go way back, and even two years ago, I'd have never bet on either one of us getting domesticated, but yeah…Ty is my forever." He laughed a little. "I don't know why you picked Lisa, but I understand being ready to find…someone. I even understand why you think it needs to be a woman."

"Cass, I'm bisexual, but we both know America isn't ready for one of their country music stars to date another man. Tim would have a fucking heart attack trying to deal with all the publicity and cancelled bookings."

Cass shrugged. "I don't think it's near the catastrophe you and your manager seem to think. Hell, it was a non-event when Anderson Cooper came out. Ellen, Zachary Quinto, Neil Patrick Harris, Matt Bohmer, Adam Lambert. It's a long list these days. They've opened the door. It's up to you whether you want to step through."

Brody took another long drink, forcing himself to wait before he responded, but the words still sounded harsh. "I think it's easy for you to say, sitting here in the middle of nowhere, surrounded by a bunch of gay cowboys. You might forget, I make my money selling music to mainstream America—not the American Idol crowd. Country music fans aren't generally known for being the most liberal." He shrugged. "It's not like I'm suffering. I love women, too, so it just makes life easier."

"Easier to ignore when someone like Whit walks into your life?" Cass held up a hand to forestall another reply. "I'll mind my own business. For now. You come by later and meet Ty. I've got to go find Whit and tell him there's a change in his duties."

I don't want a thing. Except you.

Whit's words from the night before whispered through Brody. "Cass, really. Having him with me constantly is going to be a problem for both of us. I need some space. I'm—I'm writing music again. That hasn't happened in a long time."

The tall cowboy stared at his bottle, as if looking for an answer to a difficult problem. "All right. He can stick to most of his regular duties in the compound. But I want him always within sight of the casita or you. If you decide it has to be a different ranch hand, then I'll find one, but it's going to be *someone* until after the Ranch Quest event. And he's staying here at night. Not negotiable. Unless you want to stay in the main house."

Chapter Eight

Whit walked toward the casita with all the enthusiasm of a man going to his own surprise party. Or the gallows. He knew something was coming, just not what.

"Just give him some time, Whit. If it's right, it'll work out." Cass's words had been meant as encouraging—and what the hell could he say to that? His boss assured him the assignment was genuine. Brody *did* need someone around who was smart enough to deal with rat bastard reporters, someone with absolute discretion, and someone Cass could count on to have Brody's best interest in mind.

The skittish singer knew Whit was "assigned" to run interference—that didn't mean he would be happy about it.

Whit automatically scanned the surroundings as he crossed the compound, his mind working the problem of Brody's safety. The chores for the day were finished. The debris from the storm cleaned up, the compound re-graded. Most of the other ranch hands were heading to the main house for dinner, and no one else was on-site. Not that the day-to-day residents would be a problem. Hell, it probably couldn't get much more security conscious out here. The new cameras had been installed in the wake of the previous sabotage, and they had a former Navy SEAL, a former federal law enforcement officer, and the former sheriff all employed at the ranch. And just because they were 'former' didn't mean they weren't still badass as all hell. But all the knife-throwing, gun-wielding bad-assery might be a bit of overkill when dealing with members of the press. Particularly for someone like Brody Kent, who presumably still valued his career. It would be up to Whit to keep alert, watching for a cat among the pigeons as the saying goes—once the people from the outside started to arrive.

Time for total honesty with himself. Any complaints about his temporary duties and living arrangements were nothing more than a smokescreen. He'd fallen—fallen hard. It didn't matter that he'd only been around Brody for a day…hadn't he carried a piece of him in his heart for years? Brody Kent was his first crush—the first time Whit had known for certain he liked boys instead of girls.

From the moment he'd heard Brody was coming to stay at the WSR, Whit had tried to stomp down hard on the little thrill of excitement and sick resentment he always felt when he thought about Brody. He'd thought he'd prepared for the impact of the grown man instead of the teenager. He'd been wrong. Even if the bolt of lightning during the storm was unrelated, the impact was the same. An electric strike to the heart.

Whit hesitated on the porch, stuck between knocking and just walking in. Technically, he lived here for the time being...

The sound of a guitar carried through the open windows, the same song he'd watched Brody writing yesterday, the notes already familiar, a new favorite. Whit quietly turned the knob and stepped inside. Brody was seated on the big leather couch, his eyes closed, fingers working the strings, lips moving. Whit closed the door and leaned back, content to watch and listen.

Today, Brody didn't hesitate over the notes, didn't stop and start, just played straight through, singing softly under his breath, and Whit wished he could hear the words. The melody built to a thundering crescendo. Brody opened his eyes, his gaze unerringly locked on Whit's as the refrain picked up once more. A quiet, happy sound that stirred a warm feeling somewhere in the vicinity of his heart. Or maybe that was the look Brody gave him.

When Brody finished the song, Whit applauded. For just a moment there was a look of surprised pleasure, a smile that reached those beautiful green eyes. Then as if someone pulled down the shades, the smile faded, his lids lowered.

"Hey, that was really good. That's the song you were working on yesterday, right?" Whit asked, hoping to bring the smile back.

Brody nodded. "I…uh…I haven't written much in a while," he said. His voice rose at the end, as if it was a question. He sounded unsure of himself. "I'll have to call Tim tomorrow, see what he thinks."

"Well, I really like it, if that counts for anything. I don't actually know much about the music industry. Tim's your manager, right? Does he have to approve all your music or something?"

Brody smiled. "Technically no. But we've worked together since the beginning, and he's got a pretty good ear for what will sell and what won't." Again the smile slipped away. "If he tells me it's not ready, then it'll join the others in the junk pile."

Whit frowned. Crossing the room, he joined Brody on the couch. "Like I said, I don't know much about the industry, but it seems to me, any song by Brody Kent would be well-received. I definitely know what I just heard was good. Really good."

The smile returned, brighter than before. "'In a Good Way,'" Brody said. His voice held a hint of the refrain, and Whit realized that must be the title.

"Sing it for me?" Whit asked. "I mean with the words?"

Brody shook his head. "Not yet. Let me sit on it tonight—let it settle. I really just finished when you came in."

"Sorry, I didn't mean to disturb you." Whit started to rise, but Brody put a hand on his arm to hold him in place.

"You didn't. I actually expected you earlier, given Cass's insistence. Do you mind? I mean, it's probably damn insulting for you to be asked to babysit me."

Brody's touch was hot, the calloused fingers pressing into his skin, and he leaned closer as he spoke. His gaze seemed to rake over Whit's face, and they stared at each other, separated by less than a foot. Brody wet his lips, and Whit stared. The signals Brody sent out were mixed—but there was no doubt he was attracted. Whit would have known even without last night's mind-drugging kisses, the hard body pressed against his, the smooth feel of scalp beneath his palm. Would have known without the quickened breath and the way his fingers tightened just now.

There was just something between them that demanded exploring. He wanted nothing more than to pull Brody into another of those long, slow kisses, to see where it might lead.

Oh boy. Whit had been trying to push that thought from his mind for the past several hours. Until he knew for sure Brody was safe. There were two bedrooms. A long, cold shower and maybe there was a game on TV. It didn't matter which sport, just something to stare at besides this sex-on-a-stick temptation.

Whit eased his arm from Brody's grip. "Let me wash up, and we can go to the main house for dinner."

"I admit, I really enjoyed the solitude of your place. I don't—I'm not ready to be around everyone tonight, Whit. There's a shitload of food in the fridge. You go ahead—I'm gonna have a sandwich. I'll be all right here alone."

"That's not a problem for me. I'll make us a couple of sandwiches and—"

"Why are you being so nice to me? We're not gonna…you know…"

Whit laughed out loud, his good intentions flying straight out the window. "We're not gonna…you know? *You know?*"

Brody grinned back, his cheeks flushed. "We're not going to fuck. Is that better?"

Whit's smile faded. "No," he said honestly. "That's not better at all. We can call it make love, if you prefer. But yeah…we are. I think we're going to do exactly that. Eventually. I'll wait."

Chapter Nine

Brody watched open-mouthed as Whit sauntered toward the kitchen. Really? *He'd wait?* What the hell was he supposed to do with that thought playing pinball in his brain? He closed his eyes, trying to erase the enticing view of the slim hips encased in denim as Whit walked away. Instead of making things better, he was treated to the memory of the pale ass cheeks he'd spied yesterday when Whit stripped from his wet clothes. *Jesus-fucking-Christ.*

Jumping to his feet, Brody propped his guitar against the case and stomped into the kitchen. Whit's head was inside the refrigerator as he gathered the fixings for sandwiches. "Do you like ham or roast beef?"

"Why are you doing this?" Brody demanded again.

"Doing what? Making dinner?" Whit straightened and let the fridge door swing closed.

"Being so nice to me. Is this what you do?"

"What I do?" Whit wore a half-smile. The son of a bitch knew damned good and well he'd gotten under Brody's skin.

"Rescuing people? Seducing strangers."

Whit's smile broadened. "Is that what you think this is about? Me rescuing you? I'm not interested in being Sir Galahad. And…" He brushed his fingers along Brody's arm for a moment. "I told you already, you're not a stranger."

"What? You think you know me? You and my other ten thousand closest fans?" Brody was surprised at the bitterness of his words. "The same fans who'll turn their backs if I get caught with another man? Fuck you. You don't know shit." He pushed against the bigger man's chest, so angry now he wanted to hit something. Someone. Preferably Whit.

"Hold that thought." Whit reached around Brody and twisted the little rod hanging from the blinds over the sink, closing them tight against the late afternoon light. Then with his whole body, he forced Brody backward, pinning him against the counter, towering over him, and pissing him off even more.

Brody shoved at the broad chest, rocking Whit on his feet, but not moving him even half a step. "Back off."

"Yes…I know you. At least— How many people named Whit have you known in your life?" Whit growled the question, his body tight with tension, clearly not ready to back off as requested.

"I've *never* met anyone named Whit…" He frowned as a memory niggled. "Not unless you count some scrawny twelve-year-old friend of my brother's a hundred years ago."

"Actually, I was fifteen the last time you saw me, but who's counting?"

The counter cut into Brody's back as he leaned away to get a clear look at Whit's face, trying to see past the brush of beard, the laugh lines, the square jaw. Was it possible the soft-faced…kid…was in there? Whit's jaw tightened when Brody said nothing.

"When I *was* twelve," he bit out, "one look at you in your tightie-whities as you sauntered across the hall to the bathroom was enough to confirm which team I wanted to play for. Later that year, it was the thought of your face combined with my right hand that gave me my first orgasm. When I was thirteen, you played your first song for me and your brother Max. You liked us to hang out in the garage and watch you play. And with every new song, you wormed your way further into my *scrawny* heart."

Brody shook his head, as if he could refute Whit's words.

Whit wrapped his hand around the back of Brody's head, halting the silent denial. "When you left home to be a star, you took my heart with you. You want to say I don't know you—fair enough, but I know you well enough to know which songs are personal and which are just music. I knew Lisa Bennington could never give you what you need."

Whit's gaze dropped to Brody's mouth when he sucked in a shaky breath. His tongue darted out to moisten his lips, and he knew he was sending out mixed signals, but damn…Whit's anger was hot.

"You want to know the irony, Brody? Two days ago, I was steeling myself to see you, because I knew you were headed to the WSR. I thought I loved you and maybe hated you in equal measure. My first love and my first broken heart, and you had no idea. Then that reporter chased you onto my land, and because no one was around—just you and me—I think maybe we both had a chance to see each other in a way that wouldn't have happened if we'd met here."

"And now—do you still..." The half-question came out as a whisper, but Brody couldn't stop himself from asking.

"Now that I've had a taste? Had you in my arms? Every feeling I had before yesterday pales in comparison." He tilted Brody's head, leaned down until only a breath separated their lips. "I can see it in your eyes, feel it in every line of your body. You want me, too. You said it yourself yesterday. *This is inevitable.*" Then Whit claimed his mouth, and Brody discovered the true meaning of lost.

Whit's mouth was hot as he kissed the breath from his lungs, leaning closer to press his leg between Brody's thighs. Brody thrust back, his hips rubbing against the taller man's leg, damning the clothes that separated them. Whit smelled like leather and sweat and horse—with an underlying scent that was all him. The most intoxicating aroma on the planet.

"Brody." His name was a whisper of need from Whit's lips, and Brody could almost shoot from the sound alone—that was how strongly Whit's desire affected him. As quickly as it started, Whit dropped his hands to Brody's waist and took half a step back.

His knees practically buckled, but he wasn't sure if it was from the loss of contact or relief. But relief from what? That he wouldn't have to make a decision? Was there any real question about what they would do?

Years of always living in the spotlight had hardened him, left callouses around his heart and taught him to guard his feelings. That was partly what made the idea of a marriage to Lisa seem perfect. They might not have been passionately in love with each other, but he'd honestly believed that as a rising star, she'd had nearly as much too lose as he had. It might be a sad commentary on celebrity life, but it was a fact—and showed her betrayal in true light. Over the last few weeks, he'd come to realize, Lisa Bennington was a celebrity—famous for being famous. She planned to use whatever she could to turn her fifteen minutes of fame into something bigger. The pre-nup and non-disclosure agreements might save him, but in the long run, he'd probably end up paying her anyway, because the only other alternative would be to take her to court…and his life would become evidence against him. He'd win the case but lose in the court of public opinion.

As if he'd followed the inner dialogue and sought to offer comfort, Whit traced a finger along Brody's cheek. "I won't take what you aren't ready to give. We don't have to do a thing, and I'll still keep you safe. I want you, Brody, but I think—"

Dropping the gentle caress, Whit chewed his lip, then took a deep breath as if steeling himself for rejection. "You asked me last night if I listened to your music, and I do. But I'd listen to your music if the only place you ever played was my front porch and not another soul in the world heard it. I listen because it's part of you, it's part of who you are." He dropped his hand.

"I know you've been hurt. I know there are people out there who want to use you for their own gain or fame. They want to climb on your star and ride it across the sky. But the minute a bigger, brighter star passes, they'd jump—always looking for the next rush. It's like—I don't know—fame by proxy?"

Brody nodded. That was exactly what it was like.

"I'm not one of them. If that was all I wanted, then I could have used my old friendship with your brother Max and contacted you any time over the last fifteen years. I never saw the point. You hadn't noticed me when we were teens, and there was no reason to expect that would change. No reason for you to be interested in someone like me. You're a big star—all over the press with beautiful women. I'm the total opposite in just about every way. I'm a homebody, content to work the land, ride horses, and shovel shit. All I want to do is work here to save up money for my own place—"

"You've got that now," Brody said.

Whit shook his head. "Not quite. I've got a start. Some land. The house needs some serious attention or a complete overhaul…haven't decided which. I want a barn, horses. Just enough to call it home. I guess—" He rubbed his hand in his hair, leaving it sticking up in the back. "Did I just talk you out of this? Because that would be messed up. Not what I meant to do at all. I want to be with you, but I know—" Whit stopped talking and let his hands fall to his sides. In a strained voice that seemed to settle right around Brody's groin, Whit added, "I know you're worried—but just for tonight, stop worrying, stop thinking. What happens here is just between us. Let me make love to you."

Brody opened his mouth to say…something. Anything—but all his words were gone. All that remained was an overwhelming need to feel Whit wrapped around him, inside him. To taste. To hold. To explore every inch of that big hard cowboy standing in front of him. Whit's eyes were dark with desire, heavy with need. He'd laid his soul bare, asked for what he wanted, and then handed the power of yes or no to Brody.

Could he trust Whit? The very air around them seemed alive with the answer. *Yes.*

His shields all but demolished, Brody closed his mouth without saying a word, then nodded. Once.

Whit slid one hand along his scalp to cup the back of his head, the other beneath his hips, to press them firmly together. Whit's mouth was hot, yet surprisingly gentle—the first desperate rush turning into a savoring sweetness. Whit tasted every inch of Brody's lips, pressing soft kisses into the corners, his tongue swiping over the curves, then rasping along his five o'clock shadow. Savoring. Prolonging the moment, filling them both with anticipation. His entire body seemed at odds with itself. Soft and pliant as he leaned in to take the gentle kisses. Hard and unyielding where his cock nearly strangled against his zipper.

"Please," he whispered, when Whit finally raised his head so they could gulp in air. "I need—"

The words dried upon his tongue, but Whit seemed to understand.

"Will you trust me?" Whit asked, his dark eyes heavy with desire.

"Yes." The word hissed out on a sigh.

"Go to your bedroom. I'll be there in a minute."

Brody searched Whit's face and got a half-smile from those kiss-swollen lips. "Go on. I'm going to close things up tight." Before he turned away to let Brody out from against the counter, Whit took his mouth once more and kissed him until his legs threatened to give way. "Go," he murmured, his breath a whisper across Brody's lips.

A long moment after Whit walked toward the living room to draw the blinds, Brody pushed off the counter and walked stiffly toward his room. *Very stiffly.*

Chapter Ten

Whit resisted the urge to check the windows and doors a third time, and instead went to the room containing his overnight bags. He rummaged until he located his shaving kit, and removed the little bottle of lube, but had to take nearly everything out before he found a strip of condoms. As tempting as it was to race after Brody, he caught a whiff of horse and sweat. He'd come straight in from an afternoon of work and smelled like it. Good lord, he'd been all over the man. He was lucky Brody hadn't passed out.

After stripping off his clothes, Whit took the world's fastest shower, wincing slightly as he passed the soap over his cock. God, if he just rubbed a quick one out first... Groaning aloud at the temptation, Whit rinsed, then turned off the water. Quickly drying himself, he wrapped the towel around his waist, retrieved his supplies, then practically race-walked down the hall. The door to the bedroom was partially closed, and Whit knocked softly before opening it. The sound of the shower running told its own story, so Whit checked the windows and blinds in Brody's room to be doubly sure no one could see inside. He wasn't worried about anyone who lived on the ranch.

All the other casitas were occupied by couples. Closed blinds screamed "Do not disturb."

After a moment's hesitation, Whit folded back the sheets, plumped the pillows, then, still wearing his towel, he lay on the far side of the bed, so he could watch Brody approach, and judge his continued willingness. Neither of them were virgins...not by a long shot. But Brody had an air about him, something that for all his self-assurance on the stage and in crowds that felt shy, skittish. As badly as Whit wanted this night together—he wanted more. A lot more. He wouldn't risk this shot at his future for a single night of fucking. Brody had to come to him.

The water shut off, and a heartbeat later, the door opened and Brody Kent stepped from the bathroom. Like him, Brody wore nothing but a towel. His chest was smooth, golden, seeming to match the tiny gold hoops that pierced his nipples. He'd known they were there, caught hints of them through Brody's T-shirts and seen press photos over the years. God, he wanted to taste every inch. He swallowed hard as he followed the path of a single drop of water trailing down the well-defined muscles and flat stomach. The earthy smell of herbal soap carried on the steam billowing from the bathroom. Whit sucked in a breath at the perfection of the other man.

Brody flashed a practiced smile, teased at the corner of his towel, then sauntered across the room, the steps sure, hips swinging.

Disappointment flooded through Whit as he pushed himself up from the bed and turned away. "You get dressed while I go finish fixing us some dinner."

Brody bounced on the bed behind him and tugged at Whit's towel just as he stepped away, and the knot at his waist slid loose, leaving him naked and exposed. Brody made a show of licking his lips and waggled his brows. "I'm hungry, but not for dinner. Why don't you bring that piece of meat over here?"

"Stop it," Whit said quietly. Apparently unconcerned with the conflict in Whit's heart, his cock acted like a Brody Kent divining rod, pointing straight at the object of his desire.

Brody rose up on his knees and began to jack himself with a lazy hand. His gaze dropped to Whit's dick. "Come on, honey. Let's make a special memory."

"Is that what you tell all the groupies? 'Cause I gotta tell you, it doesn't do shit for me. In fact"— Whit turned, giving Brody a good look at his bare ass as he headed toward the bedroom door—"all this little act of yours does is remind me that I was gonna have a bologna sandwich."

Brody sputtered and might have still been talking when Whit strode out, but he didn't stick around to hear.

Whit's momentary hurt had quickly given way— first, to humiliation and then to anger. *Note to self:*

Brody Kent is a big fucking star—got that, fuck you very much.

Regardless of their connection, Brody'd deliberately tried to make Whit feel like one of the legion who'd been given the "honor" of having sex with him.

Returning to his room, Whit dragged on a pair of shorts and a T-shirt from his bag. After a moment's hesitation, he unpacked his clothes, putting the contents into the dresser. Keeping Brody safe was still his highest priority, and some careless words—or a misplaced shield—didn't change how he felt about the man. There were plenty of reasons he behaved as he did, even if Whit didn't like it—but that didn't mean he had to accept being treated as…a piece of meat, either.

Skittish, hurt, gun-shy…however you wanted to try to characterize the emotions behind the way he'd behaved, Brody had made his choice. He'd been ready to give in to his desire to have sex with Whit, but still had wanted to relegate it to a meaningless act, nothing more than scratching an itch. A physical release he could get from his hand or any other willing receptacle. It was about time someone made him see there were consequences behind his actions. There were no free passes in life.

Whit would not play the short course here. He wouldn't be one of the adoring fans or play the role of a yes-man. There was a real man beneath all of Brody's bravado and public posturing—a man with feelings he kept hidden away, except when they escaped into his music. That was the man Whit wanted to know more about—the grown-up version of the first boy he'd loved. That was a man worth fighting for. Worth waiting for. And if he gave in and fucked Brody while he was putting on the false front—well, that would make Whit no better than all the others.

Chapter Eleven

The casita had a small ramp, making it accessible to someone in a wheelchair, but Brody used the slight incline as a bench of sorts, and sat with his elbows propped on his knees, a mug of coffee cradled between his hands. The ranch had come to life hours ago, dragging Brody awake, and leaving him surprisingly enthusiastic about the day ahead. Like the coward he was though, Brody had stayed inside, away from any prying eyes, especially the dark brown eyes that had haunted his dreams once he'd descended into a fitful sleep.

Last night after Whit had stormed out—showing a very impressive tight ass on the way—*thank you very much*—Brody had in turns been pissed off, horny, and sulky. No way was Brody Kent going to chase after a piece of ass. So he'd lain naked on the big bed, listening to slamming drawers and heavy footsteps as Whit had continued about his business. He'd been certain Whit's hissy fit would burn off and the cowboy would come knocking, ready to crawl into Brody's bed and give him the ass reaming he craved.

Two full hours later, the casita had grown still in the way a house did in the middle of the night when everyone slept and Brody finally had to admit defeat. Whit had called his bluff.

As much as he'd wanted to hold on to his mad in the light of day, Brody couldn't blame Whit for walking out. For years he'd been complaining that the groupies and star chasers had reduced him to nothing more than a piece of meat—and then he'd tried to put Whit in the same category. He'd been an ass.

Despite the way they'd ended the night, there'd been a nearly full pot of coffee waiting for him when he'd shuffled from the bedroom after he heard Whit leave. And from the moment the men started moving around the compound, Whit had never left sight of the casita. Was that Whit's way of keeping Brody safe? Or maybe Cass had ordered his ranch hand to stick around. That thought sat uncomfortably. He'd liked the way Whit made him feel special because of who he really was…not because of his music career.

Brody set his empty cup aside, stretched his legs out, and leaned back against the railing, pretending he was watching all the comings and goings. He actually was having a hard time looking at anything or anyone for more than a couple of minutes before his gaze drifted back to see what Whit was doing, as if returning to its personal magnetic north.

Whit's morning had been busy. Although the hard-packed ground looked freshly graded when they'd driven in yesterday, he'd spent at least an hour driving a tractor with a front blade, smoothing barely perceivable bumps and ruts. Every few minutes he'd hop down, haul a wheelbarrow of fill dirt over, and scoop a few shovelfuls into dips and dents.

Now Whit stood in the back of a flatbed trailer hitched to his truck, catching bales of hay tossed to him from the double doors at the top of the barn. The man in the barn wore jeans and a long-sleeved deep green shirt, but no hat—probably easier working up in the loft. The two men worked in a steady rhythm. Every minute or so, he'd muscle a bale of hay through the opening let it dangle by the baling wire, then Whit would whistle through his teeth, signaling his readiness. Whit stood with his feet shoulder-width apart, knees slightly bent, arms outstretched. As each bale was sent his way, he caught the weight of the load against his chest and lowered it to the bed of the trailer in one fluid movement. He wasn't actually catching the entire weight on his arms, but more like breaking the fall.

It was punishing work that would leave most men sucking for breath, but Whit and his companion shared an easy camaraderie, their jokes and laughter breaking up the quiet of the yard. Brody watched for a while, admiring the way Whit's thigh muscles bulged and tensed in his Wranglers every time he bent to move another bulky rectangle of the hay. Too bad Whit needed the long-sleeved chambray shirt to protect his arms, because it would be something to see all that lean muscle and golden skin working shirtless.

Brody moaned softly, but he must have made more noise than he thought. Whit muscled another bale against the far side of the trailer, then turned to face Brody as he straightened. It wasn't as if his presence could be a surprise. Whit had glanced over at him more than once throughout the morning. This time, however, Whit's focused look in his direction also drew the attention of the man in the hayloft.

Brody raised his arm in what he hoped was a casual wave.

"Hey, Brody. Why don't you come on over here?" Whit shouted.

Pushing to his feet, Brody gave himself a minute to compose his features and to remind his dick to settle down. He pressed his white Stetson farther down on his forehead, in his trademark style.

There might have been horses in his neighborhood when he grew up, but that didn't make him a cowboy. He'd never felt that lack of experience more keenly than this morning as he watched Cass's ranch hands saddle up and head about their business. *Until now.*

With Whit and the unnamed cowboy watching as he crossed the dirt yard, he tried to keep from looking like he was putting on a show. *Fuck.* It was like he'd forgotten how to just move from point A to point B. How could it possibly be so hard just to walk like a regular person and not someone crossing a stage?

"You good, Whit?"

Whit smiled up at the other man—and Brody bit back an urge to growl.

"Yeah, Cliff, I'm good. By the way, this here's my friend Brody—" Sharp steel blue eyes met his, then dismissed him to turn back to Whit.

Brody followed Whit's gaze to peer up at the man in the loft. Although it was probably the angle from looking up—but Whit had called him Cliff—and damn if the man didn't look like his name. His short buzz cut showed liberal amounts of gray in his high and tight—making him seem far older than Whit. Brody didn't like anything at all about the way he smiled down, his attention seemingly solely focused on the trailer—like maybe he thought Whit was the special of the day. No…Brody didn't like that look one damned bit.

"Yeah? Friend?" Cliff said.

"Well, Cass's friend." Whit laughed a little, and his clarification hurt. "He's staying here a couple of weeks, too—so you might run into each other."

"Nice to meet you," Cliff said, moving forward to stand with his toes hanging right at the very edge of the opening. He didn't wear cowboy boots, but something heavy that looked more like steel-toed work boots.

"Thanks for your help—didn't mean to waylay you," Whit told Cliff.

"No worries. I appreciate the workout—next time I'll catch." The man's voice was like whiskey and smoke in a honkytonk bar and he made a noise deep in his chest that Brody guessed was supposed to be a laugh. It sounded a lot like the heavy rumble of the tractor Whit drove earlier.

Whit flushed. "I don't think—"

"I need more to do. I told that fucking sailor he's getting soft living out here," Cliff said.

"Death wish, much?" Whit laughed. "You don't want to piss Ty off." He looked over at Brody, including him in the joke. "Tyler is a former SEAL—I told you that, right?"

Brody nodded at Whit, but before he could speak, Cliff jumped from the open loft door, landing in the trailer and nearly rocking Whit off his feet. Grinning broadly, Cliff grabbed Whit's arm, keeping him upright.

"Shit, Cliff," Whit cursed, regaining his balance.

Apparently unrepentant, Cliff released Whit's arm, then vaulted over the side of the trailer. "When Ty told me I could take a working vacation, I expected something a little more…challenging than mending a fence. Come on, you promised to show me how to saddle a horse."

Before Whit responded, the sound of a slamming screen door drew everyone's attention toward the house. A dark-haired man, nearly as broad across the shoulders as Cliff, came stalking toward them, a wide grin across his face. "You're a fucking show-off, Jarhead."

Brody blinked rapidly at the vision in front of him. Black hair, blue eyes, wearing jeans and a white T-shirt. *Holy fuck.*

"Don't need to show off when it's all the real deal, squid." Cliff grabbed his crotch, all swagger and bravado.

"Bull-fucking-shit. I kicked your ass in BUD/S, and I can still kick it."

"Bring it on, fry-boy."

Brody's head swung back and forth like he was watching a testosterone tennis match. Whit sidled up to stand next to him. "Hey, Ty. This here is Brody—you know, Cass's friend? You don't mind if he comes to lunch, do you?"

Ty flashed a sheepish grin at Brody and swung around to shake his hand. "Nice to meet you, Brody. *Mi casa es su casa.* Sorry about the chest thumping. And of course you're welcome to lunch."

"Nice to meet you. I understand I have you to thank for all the supplies in the casita," Brody said. He was feeling uncharacteristically like the new kid on the block. These men were all treating him like he was…nothing special. It was refreshing. *Wasn't it?*

"Hey, Ty?" Whit said. "Do me a favor. Cass asked me to stick around to run interference for Brody—but I promised to show Cliff how to saddle a horse. Can Brody hang out with you until I get back? It'll only be about thirty minutes or so.

Ty slung an arm over Brody's shoulders, already moving back toward the house. "No problem, but you better double your estimate. That Marine is dumber than a box of rocks."

Feelings welled up in Brody such as he'd sung about yet never felt. He might as well have been one of the hay bales Cliff had dropped and stomped on. It was one thing to want to be treated like everyone else…and totally another to be dismissed as nothing more than an unpleasant chore.

"Hey, I appreciate it, but honestly, I'm going to lock myself up inside my place. I have a call to make to my manager and a song to write. I'll see you around." This time when he crossed the yard, he didn't give a shit who was looking. He cloaked himself in his stage persona and sauntered away.

Chapter Twelve

Whit knew he'd been rude earlier with the way he'd referred to Brody as Cass's friend and then tried to send him into the main house with Ty. It hadn't made him feel any better either, since Brody didn't respond to the comment. It probably didn't matter what he'd said. Hell—it was even true. He might have crushed on Brody as a boy, but the man hadn't known him. Cass Cartwright was the only reason Brody was at the WSR.

Of course, his comment *had* sent Brody running for cover, leaving Whit feeling exactly like the ass he'd been. He'd spent the rest of the afternoon working in sight of the casita, much as he had the morning, but his temporary housemate hadn't shown.

After kicking the dust from his boots, Whit turned the knob and pushed his way inside, uncertain of his welcome. He paused after closing the door, unsure of what he was waiting for. Listening to Brody work on his new song over the last couple of days had been a privilege, but tonight the casita was quiet. No, not exactly quiet. He could hear Brody talking from the bedroom and realized he must be on the phone.

Not wanting to intrude, Whit removed his boots at the front door and hung his black hat on the rack next to Brody's white Stetson. Wasn't that appropriate symbolism? Whit certainly felt like the bad guy today.

In desperate need of a shower, he walked down the hall toward his room, studiously trying to avoid eavesdropping on the phone conversation. Easier thought than done, since Brody was on speaker.

"I know you think it's good enough, Brody, but I think it could use…more work. Besides, I'm just not sure the time is right for a song like this. I think your time is better spent on something more productive. You can't just hole up and do nothing while Lisa's passing around cryptic sound bites like they were pieces of candy. You should be out there responding. I'm going to set you up for a publicity round—"

"No. I ain't gonna do that," Brody interrupted. "I'd rather just fucking retire today than go out there and face those sharks. They're just looking for a scandal. They want blood in the water and it ain't gonna be mine."

The door was open and Brody sat on the edge of his bed, elbows resting on his knees, guitar propped between his legs. His gaze caught Whit's as he walked by. His mouth turned into a grim line.

"Sorry," Whit mouthed at his inadvertent interruption and reached to close Brody's door, but got a head shake in response, so he kept on toward his own room.

The last thing he heard as he entered his own bedroom was the voice on the other end of the phone. "I'm sorry, Brody, I just don't think that song is ready—"

Whit closed his door on that comment. Heat crawled along his neck. That had to be Brody's manager, Tim. *What is it with this guy?* Whit might not be a fancy Nashville record producer, but he'd listened to a lot of music over his lifetime. The song Brody had been playing over the last few days was something special. He'd bet on it.

He stomped stiffly into his bathroom. Stripping quickly, he let his clothes fall to the floor. On autopilot, he adjusted the water and stepped into the shower. The hot water rinsed away sweat, dust, and hay. Working a good lather into his hair, he groaned a little at how sore his shoulders were when he raised his arms. Catching the hay tossed down by Cliff had been a great workout, but he'd overdone it a bit once he realized Brody was watching. And yeah, he mighta used Cliff to yank Brody's chain a little.

The problem with hurting someone you cared about, even if they hurt you first—well, it never worked out right for anyone. Brody's over-the-top porn opening act last night had hurt Whit's feelings. So fucking what? Given the circumstances of his life, could he really blame the man for being afraid to trust a relative stranger? *Hell no.*

Now that he'd had the dubious honor of overhearing Brody's conversation with his manager tonight, the truth behind Brody's isolated existence became even more of a reality. Over the last two days, it seemed as if everything he heard about Tim and his decisions regarding Brody's career were designed to hold him back. Or throw him off track. Something about the guy seemed off.

Of course since he hadn't actually met him, maybe he was letting his imagination run a little. Or maybe he was jealous as hell. Were Brody and Tim fuck buddies? If so, how long ago? Evidently before Tim sent Brody off to Mexico where he conveniently met the future Mrs. Three-day-wonder.

Funny how the press managed to keep finding Brody, too. Sure he was a big enough star to be recognized when he wore his trademark hat low on his forehead, the tight blue jeans, and white T-shirt. Whit didn't know shit about being a celebrity, but sunglasses, a ball cap, polo shirt, and khakis should make most people look past Brody—as long as they weren't expecting to find him. They were supposed to believe that somewhere between Prescott and Kingman a random person spotted Brody, called the press, who managed to get a reporter onto the road leading to the WSR? *Bull-fucking-shit.*

Was Tim the only one who knew of Brody's plans? There was no reason for Lisa to know, but who else might have the information? Did Brody have a publicist or other staff? Maybe he should ask Brody a few questions—if the man was still talking to him.

Whit turned off the shower and stepped out to dry off. Wrapping the large white towel around his waist, he stepped from his bathroom. He blinked in surprise. Brody Kent sat on the edge of Whit's bed in much the same position he'd adopted in the other room. Hunched over, elbows on his knees, hands clasped together. His scalp and jaw looked freshly shaved, and he wore a pair of shorts and a white T-shirt, his bare feet pale against the terra cotta tile floor.

Without straightening, he tilted his face up to look at Whit. Brody's eyes seemed a deeper green, his mouth turned down. "I'm sorry for what I did last night. Can we start over?"

That wasn't the first time Brody had asked him to start over. Didn't he know he'd had him from the first hello? Whit smiled.

"I don't think I want to start over," Whit said.

Brody nodded slowly, his shoulders slumped, giving him a resigned look, and Whit realized he'd misunderstood—Brody didn't believe Whit would give him another chance. Moving across the floor, he went to his knees directly in front of Brody.

"If we start over, I have to wait to do this." He cupped Brody's face in his hands and captured his mouth in a chaste kiss, a gentle brush of lips.

If there was a taste to sad, it was held within this kiss. Something about Brody felt broken in a way he hadn't been yesterday. There had been too many defeats recently. His failed attempt at a marriage, trying to find a few days of peace without the press, and now another rejection of a song by his manager. A man who should be moving heaven and earth to make Brody happy...

Whit had played his own part in this as well. Yesterday, Brody had finally given in to the desire to be with Whit—despite what he truly believed was a complete risk to his career. His act when he'd come out of the shower had been a way to deal with his nerves. Whit had been an ass to give up so easily. Brody deserved both his understanding and his effort. He should have called bullshit and forced Brody to talk it out. Instead, he'd let his own disappointment get in the way.

Whit wanted to kiss Brody until he found the smile from yesterday, so he kissed him again. He kept it gentle and slow, and when Whit pressed his tongue forward, Brody opened for him. They kissed until lack of oxygen forced them to pull back, gasping for air.

"Still want to start over—or can we keep going from where we left off last night?"

Brody smiled, the curve reaching up on one side and showing a deep crease in his cheek. "I...was an ass."

"You weren't the only ass in the room. I should have waited you out. I'm sorry, Brody—you are worth far more effort than I gave you. Do you forgive me?"

Brody's gaze met his, the green lighter, showing the flecks of gold he'd noticed the first time they'd been this close. Brody should always have that light in his eyes. It took Whit's breath away.

"Damn. Is that why you always wear your hat so low?" Whit murmured.

"What?" Brody asked, his voice husky.

"Your eyes. Damn, Brody. You ever need to bring someone to his knees, just flash those beautiful green eyes."

The smile widened. "Is that why you're down here?"

"No, this is why I'm down here, right now." Whit reached for the waistband of Brody's shorts and made quick work of the button and zip. Brody raised his hips, and Whit slid the shorts and underwear off together, then pushed the T-shirt out of his way. Brody tugged it over his head and tossed it aside, and suddenly, Whit had a whole lot of naked Brody Kent on his bed.

Whit wet his lips and opened wide, taking all of Brody's cock into his mouth. He swirled his tongue as he licked and opened his throat, taking the thick shaft on the first try. Just knowing he finally had Brody's cock in his mouth caused Whit's toes to curl. This was so much better than all of his dreams combined.

Brody responded immediately as Whit sucked him in; his legs splayed open wider and his hands reach forward to thread his fingers into Whit's hair.

"Holy shit, that feels so good," Brody moaned. Whit glanced at Brody's face. He looked as stunned by the pleasure as Whit felt. All Whit could do was relax his jaw and open his throat, taking every bit of the fucking Brody gave his mouth.

Twisting Whit's hair around his fingers, Brody slammed his hips upward, going deep, touching the back of his throat before sliding out to do it over and over again. Whit reached up and put two fingers into Brody's mouth. As soon as they were wet with spit, he brought them to play at the tight pucker underneath Brody's balls.

When the first finger breached Brody's hole, his thrusts became wilder, less rhythmic. The addition of the second finger drew a moan and Brody's ass clamped down at the invasion. Whit continued to work his cock with his tongue and teeth, providing distraction until Brody's ass unclenched and he started to relax.

Brody was tight, so Whit slowly withdrew his fingers, eliciting another moan. He gripped the firm ass, massaging the cheeks, separating them until he buried his face between the globes. Brody bucked and nearly yelped at the first swipe of tongue over his pucker.

"Ohgodohgodohgod…"

Whit thrust his tongue in a stabbing motion, and Brody lost his words, his head thrashing from side to side, ass chasing Whit's mouth whenever he switched to work Brody's balls. Whit loved this, loved watching Brody fall apart with pleasure. He worked the tight rim until Brody was loose and open for him.

When he judged Brody was ready, Whit lifted him by the hips, pushing him farther up onto the mattress. Following him onto the bed, Whit helped Brody flip over, so he was on all fours. He reached for the condom and lube in his nightstand drawer. Working quickly, he rolled the thin latex down his leaking cock, then flicked open the top of the bottle, liberally coating his dick, his fingers, and Brody's crease.

Keeping one hand on Brody's hip, he used the other to align himself with Brody's hole. He slapped his sheathed cock against the tight pucker, spreading the lube, and drawing more moans from Brody.

"Do it. Quit fucking teasing," Brody growled. The long line of Brody's spine stretched in front of him, and Whit traced his finger down the length before he pressed the broad tip against the tight opening. He leaned into Brody, thighs against ass, until he pushed through the ring of muscle. At once, a fine sheen of sweat coated Brody's back, and he sucked in a breath.

"God, so tight," Whit said. He soothed his hand over Brody's damp skin.

"Long time," Brody gritted. He dropped to his elbows, his ass pointing up, and forehead resting on his arms. Whit added more lube and slowly worked himself inside. In, then out, incremental inches that made him want to scream with the effort of going so slowly. As Brody's ass relaxed for him, Whit gripped his hips with both hands, moving faster, pushing forward, fitting himself fully inside.

Brody's ass was hot satin, a silky smooth sheath that squeezed and milked his cock. Whit picked up the tempo, balls slapping against balls as they rocked together, their hips working in a matching rhythm. Small grunts escaped, but Whit couldn't have said whose they were. They moved together like they were meant for each other.

God, this was something he'd always imagined, yet never in a million years thought he'd have. The reality was so much better than any childhood dream. Better than any grown-up fantasy, too. He wanted this to last, to savor every moment of their coming together.

"It's even better than I dreamed it would be," Whit confessed, his words buried against Brody's neck, as he bent down to cover his lover's back.

"What is?" Brody panted.

Whit laughed softly. "This. As if you didn't know." He slammed his hips hard, the slap of skin loud and sexy. Brody's grunt was even sexier. "I've been picturing you like this for so long."

"We've only known each other a little over three days."

"I've known you all my life—and I'm definitely doing something wrong if you're still this coherent."

Brody's answering laugh turned into a groan when Whit circled his arm around Brody's waist, his hand gripping his cock. He pistoned into Brody, his fist moving in time with his thrusts.

Neither of them tried to speak again—now it was a matter of breathing and hanging on just as long as they could.

Brody's hand clamped around Whit's, forcing him to squeeze a little harder, go faster—then he was flying as Brody's cum pumped and his ass clamped down, the spasms dragging Whit's orgasm from him. He filled Brody's ass in spurts and shudders, his face buried against the man's sweat-damp neck. He could stay right here forever. Everything about Brody Kent fit him just right.

*

"Whit…oh god…" The words spilled from his mouth and yet were so inadequate to express all that he was thinking…feeling. Whit seemed to understand, maybe even felt a little of the same magic sweeping through him. With his cock still inside Brody's ass, Whit began to lick and kiss his neck, bite along his jawline. His hot mouth closed over the sensitive skin just below Brody's earlobe, and he sucked hard, no doubt leaving a mark. He should stop him, Brody thought, even as his neck arched underneath the delicious tug of teeth and lips.

"Pulling out," Whit whispered as he freed his hand from Brody's cock, then fumbled with the condom. He tied it off and dropped it over the edge of the bed, then rolled them both to the side, so they were spooned together.

"Brody, honey? You okay?" Whit asked, wrapping him in his strong arms, a rough, calloused hand rubbing over his chest.

"Yeah," he answered, the word barely carrying on a contended sigh. The endearment should have sounded...stupid. He knew it meant less than nothing—just like when Tim called him babe, or he called all the women sugar. He tried to tell himself they hadn't done anything except a one-off. He should look at this as nothing more than fuck buddies—but he didn't want to lie. Not even to himself.

Whit continued to stroke a hand along Brody's arm, over his chest, flicking at the nipple rings. His restless mouth found new places to kiss. Taste. Suck. A hard press against Brody's ass told him they likely weren't finished, and his own cock stiffened in anticipation.

"I love this," Whit whispered quietly. "Are you too sore to go again? Or maybe this time you'd like to—"

"I'm good. Sure you're not tired of me?"

"I'll never stop wanting to touch you, Brody. Never." Whit tugged at Brody's shoulder, rolling him onto his back. "Face to face, honey. I want to see you when I'm inside.

Whit's mouth captured his, and Brody's heart thundered erratically, the pounding in his ears drowning out all semblance of common sense. Brody surrendered to Whit, unsure whether he was having a heart attack or falling in love. It didn't matter because

the result was the same, either way—a career death
sentence.

Chapter Thirteen

Whit came awake with the immediate awareness that he'd overslept. The faint glow of predawn edged the blinds in the dark bedroom, and the normal sounds of early morning ranch life confirmed his thought. With Brody draped over him like an extra blanket it was hard to think about leaving the comfort of this spot, however. He couldn't help but notice just how well they fit together in sleep as in everything else. Despite their initial challenges with trust, there wasn't any obstacle so big they couldn't work things out between them. Just the idea he was actually in love was enough to make his heart pound in a steady thwump, thwump, thwump…

Shit.

"Brody, honey? Wake up. I hear a helicopter." He was already disentangling himself as Brody came back to life. He sat up and rubbed his eyes.

"Times'it?" he slurred.

"Almost five. There ain't no fucking reason for a helo out here this early." He grabbed a pair of jeans and slipped into them, buttoning his fly as he spoke. "You awake enough? I need you to stay inside. You hear me? No peeking through the blinds, even. Just stay in this bedroom until I come back for you. Just sleep or watch TV, but whatever you do—no leaving this room. I'm going to open all the blinds on the front of the house—make it look like there's nothing to hide."

Brody seemed to catch Whit's sense of urgency. "You think it's the press," he said. It was a statement, not a question, but Whit answered anyway.

"The only other time we've had a helo out here was for emergency transport to a hospital. If that's the case, I'll come get you right away, but yeah, I think it's probably the press."

"Fuck. Goddammit all to hell anyway!" He threw a pillow across the room, then looked around as if he wanted to throw something with a little more oomph behind it. "Why can't they just leave me the fuck alone?"

Whit finished dressing, then climbed on the bed. He cupped Brody's face between his palms and planted a hard kiss on those unhappy lips. "Honey, I'm not gonna let anything bad happen. You just stay right here for a little bit and let me handle this. Then...I have an idea. Wait here for me."

Lamenting that he didn't have time to make Brody a pot of coffee, Whit raced through the casita, opening the blinds, and turning on the kitchen light. He wanted to make sure the empty interior was visible to any prying eyes. He stepped outside to find the compound full of WSR hands. They all watched as the blue and white helicopter hovered for a few minutes over the main ranch road, before finally settling on the ground with a little wobble. No one moved. They could see the pilot and his passenger looking at them through the bubble windshield.

Finally Cass raised his arm, not exactly a wave, but the signal must have seemed encouraging enough, because the engine shut down, and the rotor slowed, before finally coming to a stop.

"Brody's staying out of sight, boss," Whit said quietly. "Even if they found the connection between you—there's nothing to say he's here now."

"Agreed. You sure he'll stay hidden?"

"Yeah. I think so—as long as we get these assholes outta here in a hurry."

"That's the plan."

"You can be sure if this reporter came here, others will follow. What do you think about sending Brody back to my cabin once these assholes leave?"

"Let's get rid of these guys before we worry about the next step."

Whit nodded and waited for the show to begin. No one was better than Cass at smoothing out rough situations. His gaze strayed over closer to the main house for a moment. He saw Ty and Cliff standing, practically shoulder-to-shoulder. Their arms hung loose by their sides, and it almost looked as if they were bouncing a little on the balls of their feet. Damn. If Cass couldn't handle this situation, there might just be a couple of dead bodies to dispose of.

Chapter Fourteen

Brody looked around the dining room of the main house. Not much had changed in the years since he'd been here last—except the number of people Cass seemed to have surrounded himself with. Besides Cass, Whit, Tyler, and Cliff, he'd been introduced to Holden—a large black man who wielded his cane like it was some sort of lightsaber when he'd gotten all up in the pilot's face for landing without filing some proper paperwork or another. Next to him was Chance, a man with piercing blue eyes and a smile on his face…the better to eat you with, no doubt. Two other men—Chad and Jesse—were expected to arrive at any minute.

While they waited, people helped themselves to more coffee and several of the men filled their plates from enormous serving dishes set out on the sideboard. Whit piled a plate with fruit and cheese, grabbed a yogurt and a cup of coffee, then set the whole thing on the table in front of Brody. He gave his shoulder a reassuring squeeze and whispered in his ear, "Try to eat. I promise, everything is going to be okay." Then he straightened and moved to the other side of the room, leaving Brody feeling both bereft and relieved.

Looking down at his plate, he picked up a piece of cheese, then set it back down, untasted. He was afraid he'd puke if he tried to keep anything down. He reached for the cup of coffee. At least the caffeine might go to his bloodstream before the liquid came back up. His stomach had been roiling ever since he'd looked from the kitchen window—despite orders to stay hidden—and spotted that damned Keith Marker from TYZ.

Of all the reporters, Marker was by far the most persistent in his pursuit of everything Brody did. More than once they'd caught him digging through the trash at his estate—once he'd published a partial list of phone numbers Brody had called, causing all sorts of problems for a couple of acquaintances. Another time, Brody had been half shit-faced at a party and scrawled a couple of lines he thought would make a good song. In the light of day—and completely sober, they were crap. That didn't keep Marker from publishing a photo of the beer soaked napkin he'd used as notepaper. And although the entertainment trash weekly—or whatever the paper was called—refused to identify their source, he was pretty sure Keith was behind the nude photos captured of a starlet sunning herself on his back patio. They'd been taken only moments after Brody had been called inside to take a call, otherwise his no-nos would have been page one news, too. He hated the man with a passion.

"How did Marker find me?" Brody blurted the question, just as two more men entered through the kitchen.

Whit shrugged. "I don't think it was that hard to track you to the WSR once they had the general area you were headed toward. You and Cass have a public connection, you've been here before. I think the real question is, how did they know you were here in Arizona? Someone had to have tipped him off.

"Hey, Cass," said one of the newcomers. "We got company coming. There's a late model SUV on the main road. From the dust cloud behind him, he's in a hell of a hurry." He looked over at Brody and winked. "Good to meet you. I'm Jesse, and this here's my partner, Chad." Jesse could have stepped straight out of a Marlboro ad, but unlike the others, Chad looked a lot more like a surfer than a cowboy.

"Okay, let's talk fast, then we can tighten up any loose ends after we find out who our latest visitor is. Holden?"

"Everyone is set up, Cass. We're going to depart shortly. No one will know where Brody's going except the driver taking him."

"Now wait just a goddamn minute—" Whit interrupted, but Holden cut him off.

"Later." He barked the one word and fixed Whit with a glare. It was clear the big man didn't like it, but he clamped his lips together.

"Company's here," Ty said, peering out the window. "Male, Caucasian, five-ten, one-eighty. Mid-fifties.

"That's my manager, Tim. Tim Fichter," Brody said.

"Okay, Cass...Holden..." Whit interrupted again. "I think it's a good idea if you let Mr. Fichter in on our plans, don't you?"

They stared at each other a long moment, then Holden's lips curved into a smile. "No doubt."

Chapter Fifteen

Brody finished stuffing a week's worth of clothes in his overnight bag. The clusterfuck of a meeting was over, the plan set, and now all that was left was to say goodbye. As if that was going to be any kind of easy. He tried to avoid looking at Whit. He didn't want to see the disappointment that was evident in every word the big man uttered.

"It was my idea," Whit complained for maybe the third or fourth time.

Brody might have laughed at the plaintive tone, if it hadn't hurt so much. "It was your idea that I go somewhere else," he agreed, keeping his tone level. "I think it's probably overkill, but I trust Cass implicitly, and he trusts Holden. He said no one except the driver will know for sure where I'm headed. I don't even know which driver I'm going with—so I couldn't tell you, even if I wanted to. Besides, I had to agree to keep it from you if I wanted to maintain any peace with Tim."

It might have been sexy as hell when Whit got in Tim's face and accused him of being the leak, but the idea was ridiculous. In the middle of a very heated discussion about how to keep his privacy protected, he'd been forced to defend his manager.

At the mention of Tim's name, Whit made a growling sound that tightened things low in Brody's belly. He had to remind himself that the little thrill he felt at Whit's possessiveness wasn't a good thing. There couldn't be any type of a relationship in their future—no matter how bad he wanted it. In fact, this was the perfect opportunity to put all such foolish notions to rest—for both of them. Time for serious damage control.

"I know what you think about Tim—you made that clear enough to everybody. Dammit, Whit, he's been my manager since the very beginning. There wouldn't be a *Brody Kent* without him. He drove all the way out here as soon as he heard about the TYZ leak."

"A leak he engineered," Whit repeated stubbornly. The big man shook his head before Brody could say anything. "I don't understand why you can't see it."

Brody wanted to scream with frustration. How could he explain in a way Whit would understand his complicated relationship with Tim? "I know it seems obvious to you from the outside, but goddammit Whit, listen to me. Yes, Tim is the only one I told I was coming to the WSR. But in our world that just doesn't mean much. Reporters like Marker will dig through trash or even plant bugs if they think they can get an inside scoop. Tim's got an office with employees…it's just not as straight-forward as you think."

"It's not just this…" Whit chewed on the corner of his lip, apparently working out how to say something Brody wouldn't want to hear. "Have you considered Tim's feelings?"

"What do you mean?"

"It just seems he's—" Whit shook his head. "Maybe there's more to it than just a job for him. He's insinuated himself…not just into your record contracts, but into everything to do with your personal life. Hell, he's the one who arranged for you to be in Mexico at the same time as Lisa. And that horseshit about your song—"

"Stop, Whit. You're not making any sense. Yes, I can see how it looks, but you just don't understand the music business. Of course Tim is involved in my personal life—it's what I pay him for. He's not going to sabotage anything about my career because he earns a percentage from every dollar I make. There's nothing in it for him to expose me for sleeping with a man or deep-six a song that could be a hit."

"I'm sorry. I know you trust him. I'll stop, for now. It's just…" He raked his hand through his hair and blew out a breath. "You're leaving, and I know it's too soon for us—"

Brody's heart went into overdrive. He needed to stop this before Whit said too much…

Before he could respond, Whit closed the distance between them, the heavy hand resting on Brody's shoulder short-circuited his brain.

"Just think about it…if you asked Cass, I know he'd agree. We could leave without Tim knowing we went together, so it wouldn't cause you problems. A week alone together right now would be perfect for us. Last night—I've never felt that way about—"

"Stop," Brody managed to say. He took a deep breath and said the words that threatened to rip his own heart out. "Whit, it was special for me too, but I can't give you what you want. I can't be that forever kind of guy. Hell, I can't even go out with you in public, can't take you to an awards show, or even to McDonald's without some asshole snapping a photo and plastering it all over Twitter. Instant and infamous celebrity—that neither of us needs or wants."

"It could work." Whit said, brushing a knuckle over Brody's cheek.

He was so calm, so sure. It made Brody wish there was a way for them to be together—somewhere on the planet that no one would care if he loved a man instead of a woman. He needed to keep himself on track. Say no.

"It won't work," he said. His brain screamed at him to make it final, don't leave any wiggle room for this cowboy to think there was a chance. "I can't have a relationship like that, Whit."

Whit's smile was small and sad, but he nodded. "If the choice is to take what you're offering me—stolen moments like last night—or to walk away, I choose this. I choose you, Brody. I choose whatever you're willing to share with me, whenever you're willing to share it. I might always want to change your mind, but I–"

Brody shook his head. Oh my god…what had he said to make Whit think they could have anything other than an ending? This was a monumental disaster. Whit had to be the strong one—he had to recognize that Brody needed him to walk away for both their sakes. Anything less than a total and complete goodbye was wrong—they'd both end up hurt. Where the fuck were the words he needed to make Whit walk away? "Whit, I–"

*

Brody's face had gone pale, and Whit realized in his panic about Brody leaving, he'd managed to scare the shit out of the man. In a little over three days, Brody had gone from not wanting to admit his attraction to another man, to a full night of lovemaking. He knew Brody had felt every bit of the pull between them. He'd said it himself—they were inevitable—but this wasn't the time to remind him of that. Brody needed to be alone—needed space to breathe without someone else pressuring him into a decision. Whit would show him he would always put Brody's needs above his own.

"Whit, I–" Brody repeated.

Whit put a finger over Brody's lips. "Shh...I know you're not ready, and I know you may never be ready to give me more than this." Whit traced a hand over Brody's chest. "I won't push you. I know it sounds crazy that anyone could fall this fast—and I know that you've spent a lifetime listening to strangers tell you how much they love you. I don't know how to tell you that my feelings are real and not those of every other fan. All I can do is show you.

"If that means I have to wait—then so be it. If that means I have to watch you walk away–I can't promise I won't beg. I don't care if it makes sense or not. I can't help the way I feel—I can't stop myself from loving you."

Brody's eyes went wide at the L-word, and he pulled away, his chest rising and falling rapidly, hands clenched by his side, as he stared at Whit for a long minute. He grabbed his overnight bag with one hand and the strap for his guitar case in the other. He took one last look around the room before his gaze settled on Whit, the green eyes wide with shock. With a small shake of his head, his shoulders slumped forward, then he turned and strode away—out the door. Away from Whit. From them.

It took everything he had to watch Brody go.

Chapter Sixteen

Whit collapsed into the chair, his legs splayed, sweat-damp T-shirt clammy against his back. "Shit," he said and sat up quickly. He tugged the shirt over his head and dropped it on the floor, before reaching for the cold bottle of Corona Jesse had pressed into his hand once they'd finished for the day. He poured half the bottle down his parched throat before falling back against the chair once again. Sitting down had been a mistake—he should have gone straight for the shower, but it had seemed just a little too far to try to walk on legs that would make cooked noodles look sturdy. An eighteen-plus hour day wasn't usually enough to kick his sorry ass—but since Brody had been gone, this marked over a week of long days and sleepless nights. It had been worth it...the preparation for the Ranch Quest was complete. Tomorrow morning he would help Drew move the goats into the petting zoo the vet had set up outside the barn. Then all that would be left was to saddle a couple of the horses. Everything was perfect.

After swallowing the rest of the beer, Whit pushed to his feet and shuffled down the hall toward his bedroom. As always, his gaze went to Brody's room, an automatic glance to confirm it was both empty and the suitcases were still stacked neatly at the foot of the bed. He'd heard nothing from Brody since the caravan of trucks pulled out of the compound last week. Brody had been in the front seat of Holden's truck at the time, but Whit had no doubt the vehicles, drivers, and passengers had switched things up once they were out of sight of the compound. Whit had been left behind, ostensibly to keep an eye on Tim, to make sure Brody's manager had no opportunity to follow. It was also entirely possible he'd been kept out of the plans at Brody's request. After Whit had confessed he was falling in love, Brody'd walked away without looking back.

How had that happened in such a short time? He asked himself that each day, and despite his lack of answers, his feelings only seemed to deepen. If he could just talk to Brody, hear his voice, make sure he was okay—but he couldn't even call. Holden had been adamant that Brody leave his cell phone behind. No matter how often he'd asked for information, Holden insisted he was doing everything he could to make sure Brody got the peace and solitude he'd requested. It was hard to argue against that reasoning, because Whit would do the same.

Whit showered, then dressed in a pair of cutoff jeans before shuffling off to the kitchen for a sandwich. This would likely be his last night in the casita. Cass had requested he stay until after the Ranch Quest, but tomorrow night, he planned to sleep in his own bed in his little cabin—no matter how late they finished cleaning up.

Opening the fridge to look for lunchmeat, he was surprised to see Ty had restocked it sometime during the day. Several plastic containers were stacked on the top shelf, along with beer and sodas, plus sliced ham, roast beef, and cheese. Pulling out the top container, Whit found it full of Ty's homemade lasagna and was force to admit the cook was a god among men.

Not bothering with the microwave, Whit got a fork and carried the container to the living room. Just before he collapsed on the chair again, he remembered a drink. Backtracking, he was startled when his phone started to vibrate its way across the counter. Dreading being called back to work, he snatched the cell up, but he didn't recognize the number on the caller ID.

"Hello?"

"Hey."

"Brody? Is that you?"

"Yeah—I—I had to call."

His dinner forgotten, Whit pulled up a stool at the kitchen counter. "Honey, are you okay? Are you someplace safe?" He knew it was a stupid question as soon as he asked—neither Holden nor Cass would leave him someplace dangerous. Brody answered him anyway.

"Yeah, I am. How about you? Are you doing okay?" Brody's voice was a warm whisper, caressing over Whit's bruised heart.

"I miss you. Is that stupid? Does it bother you I said that?" Whit asked. He felt off balance, unsure of what to say.

"No. No, I like it. I just needed to hear your voice."

Brody's words set his stomach swirling and left him wanting to confess his feelings all over again. Sensing that Brody might need a little more emotional distance though, he searched for a safer topic. "We're all finished setting up for the Ranch Quest tomorrow. All that's left is the petting zoo and the pony ride," Whit said. "Well, at least for me. Ty is setting up the grills in the morning. I think he plans to stay up all night baking, too. He'll probably have five dozen cupcakes for twenty kids." He laughed. "Ty's good people. I'm sorry you didn't get to talk with him more. Maybe when you come back for your stuff."

"I got to know him a little—" Brody started then stopped abruptly. Whit realized wherever Brody was, it must have been Tyler who'd been his driver.

"Hey, no worries, I won't ask where you are, okay? And just so you know…after you left, we kept Tim here for several hours. We took his phone, too. I know you trust him…but Holden's orders were for us to maintain a complete blackout on communications and keep everyone here until you'd had plenty of time to leave the area."

"I don't know what to think about Tim—or, I suppose maybe I do, but I don't like it," Brody admitted. "I've been thinking about what you said.

This is the first time in years I've managed a week alone, without any sign whatsoever of the press. It's also the only time Tim and I have not been in contact for this long." There was a pause, and he heard Brody moving—but it was difficult to conjure a picture without knowing where he was.

"I wish I could still say with certainty Tim could be trusted. I won't condemn him without actual proof, but I'm going to be looking instead of hiding from what appears to be fact."

"I'm so sorry, honey. You deserve so much better."

Again, there was a long pause. "I'd like to see you…" Brody said.

"Maybe after the Ranch Quest? Your suitcases are still here…"

"Are you still in the casita, then?" Brody asked.

"Yeah. Cass said to stay here until after tomorrow. I think we all expect the TYZ crew or some other reporters will try to come back when the WSR is open to visitors. Not much we can do to keep them away. But maybe a few days after that. Just call me before you show up. I want to make sure I'm here."

"Are you going somewhere?"

"Yeah, I'm dragging after all the extra work this week. I plan to head to my cabin for a few days."

Brody laughed.

Whit couldn't help but smile at the happy sound. "What's so funny?"

"Oh nothing. Just returning to the scene of the crime, huh?"

"What crime is that?"

"That's where you first stole my heart..." Before Whit could react there was a loud gasp. "Shit. I gotta go. I think someone's here—"

The line disconnected. Whit looked at his phone. Call ended flashed across the screen. He thumbed the reconnect button, listening to the ringing, even as he raced to his room to slip on his flip-flops.

A recorded message informed him his party wasn't answering. "I can tell that myself, fuck you very much," he growled as he stormed out the front door of the casita. He hit redial again and ran straight for the ranch house.

Slamming through the back door without bothering to knock, he started shouting as soon as he was inside. "Cass! Ty! We've got to help Brody," he shouted loud enough to wake the dead.

"Hold up there, Whit. What's wrong?" Ty stood with a white cone shaped sleeve in his hand and a tray of cupcakes on the counter.

"Brody called. We were talking then he said someone was there. We got cut off. Come on, no fucking around, Ty, I think the reporter found him again. Where does Cass have him stashed? We've got to get there right the fuck now—"

Ty laughed and went back to piping out swirls of chocolate frosting. "Cass is there now—I'm sure that's who Brody heard." Whit squeezed his hands into fists, but left his arms hanging by his side as Ty finished the last two cupcakes.

Grabbing his phone from the counter, Ty typed in a short message. The response was almost immediate, and he smiled at whatever he read on the screen.

Meeting Whit's gaze, he said, "Yeah, they scared the shit out of Brody, but Holden and Cass are there. They brought him some more food and are just checking in. They'll be back in a little bit if you want to ask them any questions."

"Where's there?" The words seemed to squeeze out past lips that were stiff with a potent combination of anger and relief.

"Your place. That's where you suggested, right?" Ty's mouth twitched like he was trying to hold back another laugh. "Cliff and I hiked in with him. We had him in place long before his manager left the property. Cliff swears no one's been anywhere close to the cabin, except us. Trust me…he would know."

"Are you sure?"

"I would trust Cliff with my life." Ty's expression was completely serious, all signs of the teasing laughter gone.

"Would you trust him with Cass's life?"

Ty narrowed his blue eyes and stared at him a long moment. "That's the way of it, huh?" he finally asked.

Whit nodded. "Would you? If it was Cass's life on the line, I mean?"

"You mean if I was already dead so I couldn't be there myself? Yeah…I would."

Chapter Seventeen

"Brody? Mind if we come in?"

Heart thundering and pulse racing at the unexpected visit, Brody went to the front door of Whit's cabin. There wasn't any security peephole in the old door, and he couldn't see from the angle of the windows, but he recognized Cass's voice. He flung the door open to find Cass and Holden standing on the threshold. A movement near the trees caught his eye, and he watched as Cliff slipped into the woods and then disappeared from view.

"Cass! What are you doing here? Why didn't you call?"

"That was my doing," Holden answered. "I'm positive no one knows where you are at this point. I don't see how reporters could be tracking your calls, since that's a disposable phone we left you with, but I didn't see any real reason to take a chance." He flashed a smile in the direction of the woods. "Especially since we already knew you were home."

"Has someone been there watching all along?" Brody led the way inside while they spoke.

"Mostly Cliff, but some of the other guys. Someone's been around—but we left you your privacy. Whit has a good chunk of land, so we were able to stay close without hovering," Cass said.

"Thank you. I can't—well, I'm not sure I'll ever be able to thank you enough."

"You can thank us by letting us empty these backpacks," Holden said, sliding the straps from his shoulders.

Cass followed suit, and they all headed into the kitchen.

"Goddamn, that's a hell of a hike for an old man," Holden said as he removed several cans and boxes and began to stack everything on the counter.

"You're not old, just out of shape," Cass laughed. He removed an insulated bag containing frozen packages of neatly labeled meat and casseroles.

"How did that happen? Drew runs my ass all over the county when I'm not working for you."

"Behind the desk or behind the wheel," Cass answered. "It's still mostly sitting. We need to get you up and around."

Holden waggled his walking stick at Cass. "Well, I might be tired, but I made it."

Cass started to put the cold foods away, still giving Holden a hard time.

Brody realized he was smiling. He enjoyed the easy camaraderie between the two men. After talking with Whit, now seeing Holden and Cass…it made him realize just how isolated he'd been.

When they'd left the main compound at the WSR, there had been so many emotions swirling, he'd been in turns angry, hurt, and a little sick to his stomach. Their five-vehicle procession had stopped about a mile down the road and he'd moved from Holden's truck to Cass's. When they'd hit the county road, three of the trucks went north, two went south. Cass stopped the truck again, and Brody had moved to a truck with Chad, Ty, and Cliff. They drove past the entrance to Whit's property, and he'd caught a glimpse of where his car had been stuck in the mud. After another few minutes, Chad slowed, then pulled over barely long enough for the doors to open. Cliff and Ty jumped out, grabbing bags, backpacks, and his guitar. A moment later, Chad pulled away, and Brody was dragged into the cover of the woods. When he realized where they were taking him, he wanted to laugh. Or cry.

"Still with us?" Cass said, breaking into his reverie. Brody blinked back to the present and accepted the beer Cass handed him. The three men clinked bottles and drank deeply before they moved to sit in the main room. After a minute, he realized Cass was looking at him expectantly.

"Did you find what you were looking for out here?" Cass finally asked.

"Hah…million dollar question. I suppose it helps to know what you're looking for before you can know if you found it, huh?"

"Well, you wanted out of the media crush for a while…"

"Oh yes, that's been great. I have no idea what kind of a shitstorm I'll be going back to, but a week without TV or Internet? Heaven. I slept through the first two days."

"Did you get any work done or just relax?"

Did I work? Brody rubbed a palm over his scalp for a moment as he considered his answer. "It didn't seem like work, but I've written more songs this week than I've written in the last five years. That feels good."

"That's great. You know Whit went ballistic over your manager's opinion of the last song you wrote. He said the guy was full of shit…" Cass left it there between them.

Brody sighed. "I want to say Whit was wrong about Tim…"

"But?" Holden asked.

"Do you two always tag team?"

"Yes," they said in unison. They all laughed, but when Brody finished drinking from his bottle, he realized both men were watching him expectantly.

"You're not going to let me skip this part, are you?"

"No," they said.

"Tim has been with me since the beginning. He helped build my career. I'm not kidding when I tell you I wouldn't be where I am today without his help. He got me my first record contract. Signed me to concerts one step up from where I probably should have been at the time…always pushing. Looking ahead. He is damned good at what he does."

Unable to sit any longer, Brody stood and began to pace the small room. "I've spent a lot of time thinking about the things that have happened the last year or two. I got tired, Cass. Tired of the road, of the endless stream of nameless women, of always being on display. The more I resented my career, the harder Tim pushed. He was the only person I told about coming to your place. I suppose it's possible his secretary could be the leak, but somehow…"

"You think he's been informing the press and Lisa both?"

"I don't know. Lisa wasn't so…combative at first. Now everything is spinning out of control. Her attacks, the paparazzi, the gay rumors—there's zero downtime. And Tim…" He chewed on his thumbnail for a minute. "I'm really worried Tim is the one behind the spin."

"What do you want to do about it? And what are you going to do about Whit?"

"Don't know." Brody's answer was curt, but he wasn't ready to talk about the things going on in his head.

Holden cleared his throat. "You and I don't know each other, but I know Cass, and I bet he brought me along for a reason…"

"You want to investigate Tim?" Brody asked, a sick feeling growing in his stomach.

"I will if you want me to. But I'm thinking Cass's point was more personal." Holden cleared his throat, glanced at Cass who was keeping his face suspiciously blank, then turned back to Brody. "When Ty met Cass, it was sort of a thunderbolt-from-the-sky-love-at-first-glance moment romance readers like."

Holden shifted in his seat and shook his head slightly. "Drew and I...well, oil and vinegar...or maybe cats and dogs, since he's a vet. He's a bit younger than me, and has been out his whole life. I worked in law enforcement, had a former wife...and a son. One Drew didn't know about."

"Are you trying to tell me how you came out of the closet and I should too?" Brody's bitterness crept through his words.

"Hell no," Holden exclaimed. He leaned forward, elbows on his knees, walking stick in one hand, bottle of beer in the other. "No one can tell you that—because no one is in your shoes. You may never decide to say anything. It's different for every gay man or woman—every bisexual. But I do have a point you might consider." Holden stared at the bottle as if surprised to realize it was empty. He set it on the table.

"I was the sheriff of this county when I first met Drew and I was in the closet for a lot of reasons." He turned his head to give Cass a long look before he turned back to Brody. "There was an explosion. I damned near lost my life—came to find out a long time later it was Drew who'd saved me. That didn't stop us from being stupid. Drew and I walked away from each other, because neither of us was willing to bend. The reasons seemed goddamned important at the time. Eventually, with the help of a couple of pain in the ass friends—we managed to fix things before it was too late." He raised the walking stick, then let it slide through his hand. "Careers come and go for a lot of reasons, Brody," he said at last. "Love might only come around once."

Holden pushed to his feet. "I'm going to start back to the truck, Cass. My leg is starting to stiffen up. You come along whenever you're ready. No hurry."

Brody watched Holden go, then turned to find his old friend facing him. "Nice setup—I guess I get your version next?" He layered the question with a little laugh. He wasn't upset—his thoughts had followed a similar track more than once this past week.

Cass leaned back and stretched out his long legs. "Me? Nope, I don't think I have anything to add to that. Actually, I was wondering about what happens if you confirm Tim has been the leak. Are you still under contract with your record company?"

Surprised Cass wasn't pressing his advantage, Brody tried to shift back to business. "No… That's been part of my ongoing discontent and the source of some of the disagreements with Tim. I haven't liked the terms—always tied to endless rounds of concert tours and publicity." He sighed and felt unutterably weary. "If Tim is behind any of this…the press…Lisa…" He shook his head. "There is no way

I could ever trust him again. Honestly…I think we're already through."

Brody started back toward the couch, but Cass stood. "I'm gonna head out so Holden doesn't have to wait too long. You know we have the Ranch Quest tomorrow. We haven't invited any press, but I can't promise there won't be any."

"Whit said everything was all organized."

"He's worked his ass off—I'm glad you called him. Anyway…if you get a hankering to sing, I'm sure the kids would love to see you. Might make the day just that much more special."

Blinking in surprise, Brody's mouth fell open. "Really? Now you're pressuring me to come sing at this little festival you have? What kind of bullshit is that, Cass?"

The laughter was long and loud, and Brody felt the flush crawl up his neck.

"Sensitive much? No pressure at all—I just thought you might enjoy singing for folks again," Cass said. "Once upon a time, I remember you saying you liked singing in bars, county fairs, and small halls because you got to connect with the fans in a different way." He shrugged. "Might be something you hadn't considered while you're trying to figure out what to do next. I don't believe having a family and a music career are incompatible. Seemed to work fine for Garth."

Chapter Eighteen

The morning of the Ranch Quest broke bright and sunny. The compound was full of striped canopies, bright banners, and two giant barbecues. It seemed as if they'd been preparing for this day for months, and Whit knew every man on the WSR would work hard to make this the event Ty dreamed of. Like Whit, many of of the hands had lived here for years, and Cass had always treated everyone right. But from the minute Cass and Ty had become a couple, the place had felt more like a home. They were family. The only thing that could make this day better would be if Brody were by his side. He'd hoped for a call back last night, but that hadn't happened.

He watched as the big blue Chevy pickup towing a horse trailer pulled into the yard and parked alongside the area of the corral that had been sectioned off for the petting zoo.

"Hey, Whit," Drew said as he climbed from the cab. Otherwise known as Doc Van, Drew was the large animal veterinarian for this part of the county. As such, he'd have likely been by the WSR often enough anyway, if he hadn't already lived here. Drew, Holden, and their son, Alex, had actually lived in the casita where Whit was staying—until just a few weeks ago when they'd moved into their own place on a chunk of land Cass had given them.

Drew was close in age to Whit, and they got along well. There'd been more than one late-night barn call when Whit had been pressed into service as a veterinary assistant.

"Hey yourself, Drew," he said. "Where's the short one and Holden?"

Drew smiled. "Holden and Alex will be along in a few. We thought it might be better to bring two vehicles, just in case one of us has to leave in a hurry. Doctor Foster is covering for me, but you never know."

While Drew spoke, Whit moved to the trailer and began unloading Betsy, one of the Shetland ponies borrowed for the day. By the time they finished with the trailer and the WSR animals, the pen held two silky Angora rabbits, two momma goats and their two kids, a rooster, two hens, a sheep, an alpaca, and a tortoise.

"This is quite a menagerie," Whit said.

Drew laughed. "The kids will love it. We have more ponies plus the horses in the other corrals. Jesse was going to pen a couple of longhorns. I think the kids will get a good long look at whatever animals they like. From what I understand, there will be two children who won't be able to ride at all because of their conditions, so I want to make sure they get to spend as much time as they want in here."

"That's a good idea. If you have everything you need for now, I'm going to help Bryan and Chad set up the chairs and tables under the food canopy. Ty's got the grills going, drinks are on ice…I think we're good to go. The bus should be here in less than an hour."

By the time Whit arrived, the dining tent was already set up and decorated, with red and white tablecloths clipped to the rows of picnic tables. A side table was loaded with stacks of paper plates, napkins, plasticware, and bottles of condiments. Two other tables waited for the trays of food that would be carried out once it was time to serve the food. With nothing else to do at the moment, Whit wandered over to the grills.

"Hey, Ty, how's it going?"

"It's going…I can't believe we're finally here." Ty's blue eyes sparkled under his neatly trimmed black hair as he looked around at all the preparations. His white industrial apron covered his typical blue jeans and T-shirt. One of the two grills was actually a smoker, and it was loaded with both chicken and ribs. The other was for the hot dogs and hamburgers. The heavy layer of charcoal was enough to cook for several hours. The twenty or so men of the WSR could pack away the food, but he suspected the quantities Ty had going would feed a whole ship. That didn't even count all the organic fruits and veggies, and the pile of healthy side dishes. It would definitely be a week of leftovers.

"Need some help?" They must have been the words Ty was waiting to hear, because for the next little while he was busy ferrying dishes and aluminum trays of ribs and chicken from the house to the grill and back again.

A piercing whistle carried on the light breeze, and Whit looked up to see Cass waving his hat and looking around the yard. "They're five minutes out. Holden is escorting them in. Everyone take your places."

Whit fought a grin at the thrum of excitement around the yard. Men came out from the barn, the bunkhouse, and the tents, to stand in the compound to greet the kids. Every single one of the men was dressed in some sort of "cowboy duds" as Cass had called them. Jeans and cowboy hats. Boots, spurs, and holsters. Several had on vests, or had ropes hanging from a shoulder. Juan even wore his chaps. Jesse rode Angel, his devil of a horse, and would put on a real show for the kids later. Anything to add the feel of the ranch life and make this day special. It made Whit wonder who was more excited, the ranch hands or the kids?

The bus rolled into view, a long rehabbed school bus painted white, with Pinetop Stars Camp emblazoned along the side. Dust kicked up and swirled as the bus bumped over their long dirt drive.

"Tyler? Get up here," Cass hollered.

Shaking his head, Ty opened his mouth to protest, but Whit took the tongs and pushed him forward.

"Go, Ty. This is your day as much as theirs. I can manage here for a while."

The big man nodded and trotted off. He watched as the counselors unloaded first, helping the children who could walk exit from the front of the bus. Another counselor was at the rear operating the wheelchair lift. Whit didn't think a man there would admit to it, but he'd bet he wasn't the only who seemed to be having a little trouble with his eyes stinging.

The counselors, kids, and some assorted family members huddled at the front of the bus, while Cass explained the setup. Then Ty raised his arm, gesturing back toward the compound, and it was as if a starting gun had been fired. With much laughter and shouts, the kids took off in all directions.

Eventually Whit would help Jesse get ready for his show, but for now, he was content to watch as Ty and Cass walked next to the two wheelchairs, guiding them to the petting zoo. One of the kids used a hand control to drive his mechanized chair, while the other needed the help of a counselor to cross the yard.

Juan led several kids into the barn, where they would get to see the horses and then the pen with the cattle. Chance sat on a quad with a trailer of hay attached. He would be giving hayrides all afternoon. Bry and Chad handed out cups of lemonade or water to any of the guests who wandered through the dining tent. Whit did a mental roll call and realized Cliff was missing. Maybe Ranch Quest wasn't his thing and he was hiding out in the main house. He hadn't been around much at all this past week.

A truck and a few cars arrived as the morning progressed, but from where Whit stood near the grill, there was no way to tell if it was more parents who'd opted to drive themselves rather than ride the bus, or members of the press hoping to catch a story. Everyone seemed well-behaved, and at least the helicopter hadn't made a reappearance.

When Ty finally returned, they kicked the cooking into high gear, and soon the long tables were piled high with food, and the benches were full. Cowboys worked the room, stopping to talk with each child, handing out souvenir straw cowboy hats to everyone.

Cass stepped to the front of the tent and shook an enormous brass cowbell. Kids squealed and adults covered their ears, but everyone laughed. Once he had everyone's attention, he cleared his throat.

"I promise, no long speeches." He smiled. "I just want to thank you for coming all the way out here to Willow Springs Ranch and our first Ranch Quest. Hopefully just the first of many!"

Everyone clapped and there were a few hoots, but Cass waved them all to quiet. "I want to take the opportunity to thank the man behind the dream, Tyler Hardin, and all the men of the WSR for making this happen."

Another round of applause broke out as Cass exchanged a long look with Ty. Even from across the tent, their love for each other was obvious. Envy crawled through Whit's belly, leaving him missing Brody and feeling more alone than ever. How had this happened?

A ripple of noise seemed to work it's way through the crowd, and a few people turned their heads, but Cass held up his hand once more. "The camp director asked me to remind everyone that you're leaving at two-thirty. That gives you just over two more hours. Don't forget rodeo star Jesse Duran will be in our riding ring in an hour. Meanwhile…before you head back out to different activities, I'd like to give a warm welcome to a special friend of mine." He smiled in the direction of the main house, and there were several gasps of surprise. Whit followed Cass's gaze.

Wearing blue jeans and a T-shirt, his white Stetson pulled down low over his forehead, the newcomer was instantly recognizable.

"Ladies and gentlemen…Brody Kent."

Chapter Nineteen

"Hey there, how y'all doing?" Brody asked. He made eye contact with as many as he could, smiling at the expressions on the kid's faces. Most were excited but a couple were already looking over his shoulder, back at the horses or the petting zoo. That was only fair…this was a big outing for them, and he was all that was between them and the rest of their afternoon. This level of distracted enthusiasm was good for him. A man needed to remain humble.

Avoiding looking directly at the one person he craved to see, he swung his guitar up, adjusted the strap, and brushed his thumb over the strings. "How about I sing a few songs, then let you all get back to the ranch?" Without waiting for a response, he went right into "Rodeo"—the one song he was sure most of them would recognize, even if they didn't listen to country music. The up-tempo song with catchy lyrics had everyone tapping toes and bouncing on their seats. "Come on, sing it with me," he urged when he got to the refrain.

He moved through the rows of tables, always stopping next to one of the kids, never near the two reporters he'd spotted nearly as soon as he'd started singing. Their cameras flashed, but he didn't let it ruin his enjoyment. This day was for the kids.

When the first song was over, he decided to do something a little different. "You all are some of the best singers I've ever been around," he told the kids. "Let's see how you do with an old campfire song I used to sing when I was your age. Everybody sing along. If you don't know the words, then make some up—I plan to!"

People laughed, then he started. "She'll be coming 'round the mountain when she comes…"

Brody walked farther around the room as they sang verse after verse. She'd been driving six white horses…they'd all come out to greet her…and had their chicken and dumplings…until he couldn't think of one more thing to add. Kids were shouting the ending to each verse and he was completely positive not one person could actually hear him singing. His cheeks hurt from the broad grin stretching his mouth. He finally made his way to the young girl in the wheelchair. She was maybe twelve or thirteen, her smile matched his, but dark circles hung heavy under her eyes, and she was so frail, he bet she didn't weigh sixty pounds. But what caught his attention most of all was her lack of hair. She was probably undergoing some kind of chemo. He crouched down on the ground so they were eye to eye.

"Hey there," he said. "What's your name, beautiful?"

"Brandy," she said, her voice a whisper.

"Hey, Brandy, we really do match. I'm Brody…and check this out." He took his hat off and lowered his bald head to hers. They stared at each other, forehead to forehead, and he saw the tears that filled her eyes. "Shhh…it's gonna be okay, Brandy. And you know what? When your hair grows back all thick and beautiful, I'm still gonna look like this." Brandy gave him a smile that almost closed his throat.

Glancing up at the woman sitting next to the chair, he noticed the strong resemblance. "Mom?" he asked.

She nodded, her eyes were overbright, and she caught her lip between her teeth, as if to keep it from trembling.

"You can get in touch with me any time through the Willow Springs. You let me know how Brandy is doing, and when her hair is back, I want to make sure we get our picture together. You got a camera to take one now?" He waited while the mom took out her cell phone and snapped a picture. He was aware of other cameras clicking, but he gave Brandy his attention. When he stood, he removed his Stetson and placed it on Brandy's head. "That's for good luck, sweetheart. It always works for me." He bent and kissed the girl's cheek, then plucked her souvenir straw hat from the table and mashed it on his head, with a final wink at Brandy.

"Okay, one more song, then you all need to get back outside and run around. This is a new song I just wrote, and I want to dedicate it to someone special." His gaze scanned the room until they found the dark eyes of the man he was now certain he loved. There was no telling what the fallout would be from this little performance. Maybe nothing other than a good deed notched on his belt. Maybe it would drag him farther under the gossip grist. Either way, this was something he needed to do.

New songs were always carefully vetted, contracted, practiced until he could play it in his sleep, recorded, synthesized, and sometimes, released to great rounds of publicity. Not this one. His heart rate was nicely elevated as he played the opening chords.

Clearing his throat, he said, "Sometimes, you need a friend who can tell you just how far off track your life has gotten. Whit…this one's for you. I call it 'In a Good Way.'"

Although he'd announced ahead of time he'd written it for someone named Whit, Brody wasn't willing to throw all good sense to the wind. He didn't move to stand next to his lover, nor did he sing it while staring hopelessly in his direction. Their gazes met a few times, but Brody played to the room. This wasn't some grand coming out gesture—today was about the kids. When the song was finished, he noticed a few people wiping their eyes, more were smiling, and still others hopped to their feet to give him a standing ovation. He waved them on, shouted he'd stick around the rest of the afternoon if anyone wanted autographs. Then the show was over and it was time to shake hands, sign napkins, and smile, smile, smile.

Chapter Twenty

As the Ranch Quest drew to a close, all Whit wanted to do was chase after Brody and drag him back to their casita. He wanted to know about the song. *In a Good Way.* The words had been powerful…inspirational…loving. What did it mean? Anything? And why had Brody shown up here after being safely out of sight for a week? He'd had to know the risk of exposure of an appearance at a ranch known by many to be run by a bunch of gay cowboys. What had he been thinking?

The earlier concerns about the press had been justified, too. It turned out one TYZ reporter and one freelance photographer had come in with the parents. As soon as the kids had left the tent, Cliff and Ty had introduced themselves to the uninvited members of the press and escorted the men off the WSR. They had gotten one helluva story—and no doubt had been uploading photos before they'd even been off the property.

Unsure where to put all the feelings the day dredged up, Whit kept his head down and his feet moving. It had been a long day already, and they still had the basics of clean up to get through before taking on the regular evening chores. He worked to load the ponies and the animals from the petting zoo into the horse trailer, while keeping an eye on the activities at the front of the compound. Cass, Ty, Brody, and Jesse were at the bus, shaking hands with the kids and thanking all the adults for joining them.

When the last child was loaded, the four men stood shoulder to shoulder, waving at the departing bus and the assorted vehicles in their wake. It was a good thing so many of the parents were able to join their kids and the Pinetop Stars Camp. He slipped his hand around Betsy's halter. "You did good, old girl," he told the pony. He gave her an extra pat, then led her into the trailer.

"Those poor kids. I hate the helpless feeling when an animal is sick and I've done all I can. I'm not very good at waiting to see if the treatment will work," Drew said. He set the rabbit cage on the floor of the second stall in the trailer.

"I was thinking pretty much the same thing. It must be so hard on the parents. I'm glad a few could come along. Those kids were real happy today, and I gotta believe that every smile helps."

They checked to see everything in the back of the trailer was secure, before Whit latched up the back. He checked the hitch while Drew climbed in the truck and started the engine. "Looks like you're good, Drew," Whit said after the vet tapped his brake lights, then tested the turn signals.

"That's what Holden says." Drew grinned, then his expression turned more serious. "I didn't realize you and Brody were...friends," he said, obviously referring to the song.

Whit's gaze drifted back to the drive and the four men still standing there, watching the last of the guests depart. He shrugged. "We go back to high school—not a big deal." He wished he didn't feel the heat crawling up his neck. "Go on, Drew. Get these animals back where they belong so you can get home to Holden and Alex."

Drew studied him another minute. "I'm not going to get in your business—"

"But—" Whit interrupted with a laugh.

"Exactly," Drew laughed. "*But*...you saw what Holden and I went through. I was wrong to judge him just because he didn't live his life the way I lived mine. He had a lot on the line, including his fear of losing custody of Alex. I'd imagine a man like Brody might feel he has a lot to lose, too. And it's always personal...no matter who else knows."

"Cut to the chase, Drew," Whit said. "I think I need to go..." He'd spotted a vehicle on the road heading toward them, not away, and it was moving fast.

"Just don't make any rash decisions. If what I heard in that song was aimed at you...the man cares. Give him time."

The incoming vehicle blew past the men and came to a stop in front of the main house. Even though it was a different SUV than the rental he'd been driving on his last visit, Whit had no trouble recognizing the salt and pepper head when the new visitor emerged from the driver's side door. *Tim Fichter.*

He patted Drew's shoulder through the open window. "I gotta go—be safe." Turning toward the trouble, he matched his pace to Cass and the others, as they converged on Tim. It was like a bad parody of the OK Corral, but if Tim was intimidated by the armed cowboys surrounding Brody, he didn't show it.

"Is there someplace private we can talk?" Tim asked through a tight jaw. He looked as if he'd driven straight in from a business meeting. He wore rumpled slacks and a long-sleeved dress shirt. His tie was pulled loose around his neck. A suit jacket hung over the back of the passenger seat.

"Why are you here, Tim?" Brody asked. Tim was an attractive man, maybe ten years older than Brody, but the dark pouches under his eyes and deep brackets around his mouth hadn't been in evidence when he'd visited the WSR last week. He turned his mouth down into a frown.

"Maybe because this afternoon you single-handedly did more damage to your career than Lisa Bennington could ever do. If you'd just been answering your phone this past week and talked to me! We could have so easily avoided all this mess if you'd just come back with me when I asked. As it is, we're going to have to go into major damage control mode now to see if we can spin today's visit into having more to do with sick kids instead of the lifestyle going on here."

Whit had been watching Brody during Tim's rant, otherwise he might have missed the momentary tightening of his jaw that signaled his anger. The slow smile that crawled across that beautiful mouth had nothing to do with happy.

"What's the latest on Lisa, Tim?" Brody asked.

"If you bothered to check in, you'd know she's scheduled on the Today Show next week. And that's not the worst of what she's done—"

"Isn't it?" Brody cut in smoothly. He stepped forward, closing the gap so he and Tim were practically toe-to-toe. Ty moved to stand next to Brody and Cass stepped up to stand at his back. Jesse seemed to fade back, only to appear on the other side of Tim. For a moment, Brody seemed small, towered over by everyone surrounding him. Then he leaned closer, placing his hand on his manager's chest, creating a strangely intimate moment—as if his words were only for Tim.

"Come on, Brody. Let's go somewhere private. We have a lot to talk about. I'll tell you everything about Lisa…"

"Everything?" Brody practically cooed. "You should probably know we spoke last night. Lisa sends her regards."

Tim sputtered something unintelligible, but Brody spoke over him.

"Lisa told me so many things…"

"She's a liar," Tim shouted.

"Really?" gasped Brody. Then he chuckled. "Actually, I suppose she's really a better actress than Hollywood gives her credit for. You know, I really believed meeting her in Mexico was a coincidence. I believed we had so many things in common, when in fact the only real thing we shared was you."

Tim's mouth opened, then snapped shut. He cleared his throat. "Brody—I have always had your best interests at heart. Always—"

"Make sure you hit him in the stomach," Ty said. "Don't want to hurt your hand, Brody. But if you need someone to shut his mouth—I'm your guy."

"Actually," Whit said, *"I'm* his guy." He moved to stand on the other side of Brody and caught the hint of a smile.

Tim whipped a quick look at him. "Shut up. This is none of your goddamn business. Brody, get in the car right now. We're leaving. I have too much invested and you have too much at stake to stand around here playing cowboys and Indians with these assholes."

Tim's hand rose toward Brody, but Whit was faster. His fist connected with Tim's jaw, snapping the man's head back and buckling his knees. He'd likely have gone down if Jesse hadn't grabbed one of his arms to hold him in place. Spitting blood, he rubbed his jaw. Ty pulled Brody back half a step as Whit moved closer to Tim.

"Is there anything else you have to say to this guy right now, Brody?" Whit asked, grabbing the front of Tim's shirt.

"Not much, Whit." Brody stepped forward, but Whit kept his hold on the other man. "Tim…you betrayed me. I thought you were more than my manager. I believed you were my friend. You mighta had my best interests at heart when we first started, but somewhere along the way, you lost sight of what was important. You engineered this whole situation with Lisa, all the rumors…the press." Brody shook his head. "We can't go back from that. We're done. I'll have my new attorney contact you next week. Your confidentiality clause is still in place. You make one public comment about me, my music, my career—you talk to anyone—and I'll take everything you own."

"Are you fucking stupid?" Tim screeched. "You're at a goddamn ranch full of gay cowboys and you let the press get photos. You can't pull that back—you need me to spin it. Think, Brody. Jesus Christ—*think!*"

"The press saw what they saw. I've got nothing further to say to you on the subject. Now get the fuck out of here."

Brody turned toward the main house and walked away with Ty and Cass beside him. Whit twisted Tim's shirt in his fist and gave him a feral grin. "Go. Away."

Jesse met his gaze over Tim's shoulder and nodded once. Together they moved Tim into his car. For a long minute, the manager sat behind the wheel, his face slack, eyes wide. Then he turned the key with a shaking hand. As he shifted into gear and slowly rolled forward, Whit thought about following him off the property, but Jesse forestalled him with a wave.

"I got it—you go check on Brody. That was pretty devastating."

Whit nodded gratefully. Jesse went to one of the ranch trucks, and Whit trailed the other men to the house.

Once inside, he followed the sound of angry voices coming from the office. *What the fuck?*

"It's not the fucking right way to deal with this, Brody." Cass's voice carried down the hall, and he sounded royally pissed.

Knocking once on the closed office door, Whit stepped in without waiting for an invitation. Ty must have gone somewhere else once they'd come inside, because the office held just the two old friends. Cass stood with his hands balled into fists, leaning forward on his desk, his mouth a grim slash. Brody faced him, his shoulders slumped, lower lip caught between his teeth, his own arms folded across his chest. As soon as Whit stepped into the room, Brody's posture changed. He stood a little taller, dropped his arms, and plastered a picture perfect smile on his face.

"What's going on?" Whit asked.

Brody looked at Cass a long time before he turned to face Whit. "I've gotta go," he said.

"Go?" Whit repeated stupidly.

"Yeah. Obviously there are a few things I need to take care of, and I can't do it from here."

"But—" Whit didn't even know what or how to argue with that. It wasn't like they were a couple. Hell, they hadn't even talked since Brody'd shown back up today. Sure he'd dedicated a song to him, but they weren't teenagers and this wasn't the prom. He wouldn't throw himself at the man's feet and beg— no matter how much he wanted to. He nodded once. "Okay."

"Oh for fuck's safe," Cass muttered, his voice full of disgust.

"I'll…uh…be back." Brody crossed the room, his steps faltering only briefly as he passed Whit. "Really. It's all good—in a good way." Then, without a backward glance, Brody Kent walked out of Whit's life.

Chapter Twenty-one

Whit brooded. There was no other word for it, really. For a few brief shining moments he'd loved and thought he'd been loved in return. Happily ever after had lasted an entire afternoon. Probably more than some people had, and certainly more than he'd ever believed he'd have with Brody—but goddammit—it hadn't been enough.

After Brody had left, Whit had stared at Cass for a long minute, unsure of what to say…what to feel. Finally it had been Cass who'd broken the awkward silence.

"I'm sorry, Whit. What can I do?"

"Give me a week's vacation?"

"Going after him?"

"Going home."

Whit wouldn't have had any idea where to look for Brody. They'd never talked about stuff like that. As far as he knew, Brody owned a mansion somewhere in Tennessee, but he didn't know where—and with no television or Internet out here, he couldn't even say for certain that was where Brody had gone. Besides, he had Whit's number, so he'd have called if he'd wanted to talk. His parting words had been pretty clear. *I gotta go.*

From his position sprawled across the couch, he could just make out the time…nine-thirty. Thirty more minutes before he'd allow himself to go to bed. If he went any sooner he'd wake up too early. Without animals to feed, there wasn't much need to wake before sunrise, but some habits died hard.

He was tired enough to sleep where he sat. His vacation consisted of working every bit as hard on his own land as he did at the WSR, trying for total exhaustion so he could sleep without dreaming of Brody. The irony was, there were as many memories of Brody here at his cabin as anywhere. Brody had lived here for a week, left his mark on the space in a dozen different ways: angling the couch so it caught the morning sunlight; a forgotten bottle of shampoo in the bathroom; a piece of paper with songwriting notes on the screened-in porch. And the hardest one of all to ignore…climbing into bed each night was like a full body immersion in Brody Kent. His scent lingered on the pillows and sheets and Whit fell asleep each night with his senses full of Brody.

Blowing out a breath, Whit lifted the pad of paper from the cushion, and tried to focus on making his work plan for the next three months. First order of business was to bring the tractor out here. Life would be a helluva lot easier once he could drive his truck over the creek bed and up the hill.

Of course having a road to the cabin would have changed everything about the day Brody came crashing into his life. Closing his eyes again, he gave up trying to do anything else productive and surrendered to the memories. Soaking wet, forced to hike with a total stranger through the pouring rain after being chased off the road by a psycho reporter—and he was thinking about Brody again.

Giving up all hope of clearing Brody from his thoughts, he tossed the pad onto the table and leaned against the cushion. With the windows open and his eyes closed, Whit listened to the night.

At first, the sound seemed to come from so far away it was hard to say whether what he heard was music or the wind whispering through the trees. As the strum of guitar became clearer, Whit found himself smiling, but strangely reluctant to move. This was Brody's play.

The first song was nearly over by the time he realized Brody had settled by the front door. *I'd listen to your music if the only place you ever played was my front porch…it's part of who you are.*

When the strains of the next song started, Brody's voice rumbled over Whit like a sensual caress. He recognized it at once. It's all good—in a good way… Brody's words to him as he'd gone out the door. The words had been a promise—not goodbye. Why hadn't he been paying closer attention? *Maybe because my heart was in my throat?*

Whit stood and made his way to the front door as Brody's smooth baritone sang out the final refrain. It took his breath away to see Brody standing in his yard, strumming his guitar…singing just for him. He opened his mouth, but couldn't find any words worthy of the moment.

As if he knew the effect he had, Brody smiled, and his fingers danced over the strings in a complicated combination Whit hadn't heard before.

"I'm thinking of writing a new song," Brody said.

"I'm kinda fond of the last one you played."

"That old thing? Wrote it for a guy I used to know."

Whit laughed. "You don't say."

"True story. He made a huge difference in my life," Brody nodded and brushed his thumb over the strings once before going back to picking out the haunting melody.

"Hmm…should I be jealous?" Whit asked. "Of this guy, I mean. He sounds like he mighta been pretty important to you."

"He was special," Brody agreed, shrugging. "But he's old news, now. I've moved on."

"Should I invite you in?"

"Invite me in…" His gaze dropped to the guitar, and he played louder for a minute, as if working something out with the refrain. Then Brody looked up and even in the dim light spilling through the front door his eyes seemed to sparkle with excitement. When their gazes met, Whit's breath left him on a whoosh. Brody's smile faltered, but he picked up the tune once again, and sang softly.

"Invite me in…
"I never knew what I was looking for, until I saw you;
"Stay with me a while—forever won't be long enough.
"In my house, in my life, be my home.
"Invite me in…and never let me go away again."

The last words hung on the air as Brody stopped playing. He rested his hands on top of his guitar and worried at his lower lip while he watched Whit.

Unsure he'd be able to speak, Whit reached his hand out in a silent invitation. A shudder shook Brody's shoulders, then he nodded once. Raising the strap over his head, he switched the guitar to his left hand before stepping forward. When they were practically toe-to-toe in the doorway, Whit used his fingers to raise Brody's chin, loving everything he saw: the laugh lines fanning away from the overbright eyes, long lashes, the shadow of a beard. He brushed his thumb over the full lower lip and licked his own lips in anticipation.

"Stay with me, Brody. Come inside and I'll never let you go away again."

"Promise?"

"I promise. I love you, Brody. We'll find a way to make this work…let me be your home." He captured Brody's mouth in a kiss and pulled him inside. He briefly wondered if the gesture meant as much to Brody, then decided to trust his gut. It had taken a lot of effort and no small amount of courage to come back to him, to climb up the hill at night, to sing those words. Breaking their kiss as he closed the door, Whit whispered, his breath brushing over Brody's lips, "Welcome home."

*

Brody lay naked on the bed and wished he could remember every moment of how he'd gotten here, but time seemed to keep freezing then fast-forwarding, a breathless mix of anticipation as he'd climbed the hill in the dark, to the dreadful brain-numbing fear of rejection as he'd waited for Whit to open the door. For the first time in his life, he couldn't say with any certainty that he knew where he'd left his guitar. The universe had narrowed to this single moment in time with pinpoint accuracy to pierce his heart, leaving a gaping hole that could only be filled by this man. The man who loved him.

The bedroom was dark, but the scent of pine and earth floated in through the open windows, the breeze cool against his heated skin. He'd only been gone a few days, but the sheets were a familiar scratch, the pillows molding to him as if he were a long lost friend. And it was all so much better now because this time, he wasn't here alone.

Whit wrapped his fingers around Brody's wrists, lifting his arms above his head, trapping them in one big hand. He leaned in to run kisses and love bites along the sensitive skin on the undersides, trailing down to Brody's chest. His mouth latched on to a nipple and he flicked the ring with is tongue, then tugged it gently between his teeth.

"Oh, god," Brody moaned as the pull went right to his groin, and he bucked his hips, a silent entreaty for more.

"Mmm...love these, Brody. So damn sexy." He pinched the head of Brody's cock. "Ever think about a PA?" His mouth went back to work on the nipple, biting and sucking while his fingers continued to pinch and pull at the fleshy underside of his cock. He'd been drunk as shit when he'd gotten the nips done and the next day swore he'd never do anything so stupid again. Whit's wicked mouth and fingers had him ready to change his mind.

"Whatever you want," he promised recklessly.

Whit laughed. "We have a lifetime to explore...you might regret those words someday."

"Never," Brody promised.

Whit released his hands then and crawled up his body so they were face-to-face. He studied him with those dark eyes. Tired lines formed between his brows, and there were deep creases at the corners of his mouth. Brody cupped the bristled chin with his hand, his fingers caressing the strong jaw before threading into Whit's silky hair.

He met his lover's steady gaze, knowing their shared fears would fade over time. "I'm here for as long as you'll have me."

Whit caught his mouth in a kiss that felt like forever. Their tongues slid together, the dance becoming more familiar with every stroke. When he heard the snick of the plastic lid, Brody clung tighter to Whit's hair, but opened his legs, giving easy access. The lube was cool but the kisses stayed hot as Whit worked in one finger, then two. When they broke for air, Brody whispered a demand. "Now."

Whit withdrew his fingers, then snaked an arm underneath Brody to roll them over. Brody scooted back to straddle Whit's thighs and reached for the condom packet on the mattress. He quickly sheathed the weeping shaft, then poured lube in his palm. He jacked him a few strokes before moving forward to position himself over the heavy cock.

With a pair of big hands on his hips, Whit helped to keep him steady while Brody took a long moment to explore Whit with his eyes—the tight stomach rippled with muscles, the way his biceps and triceps bulged, the ruggedly handsome face—all so very different from what he'd ever imagined forever would look like. Yet so very perfect. He slowly lowered himself, enjoying the stretch and burn, the sense of completion he felt as Whit filled him.

As they began to rock together, he realized sex wasn't just sex anymore. Something so much bigger was happening—something utterly interconnected to a part of his heart he'd thought was missing.

"You feel so good…so right," Brody gasped.

"So damn good," Whit agreed.

Brody propped his hands on Whit's shoulders and rode his cowboy until his thigh muscles screamed and Whit was driving into him, farther, deeper, faster. He became aware of every little sensation. Their naked bodies slid against each other, the skin-to-skin contact, the feel of Whit, hot and hard, his own ass muscles as he clenched and relaxed with each stroke. Sweat trickled down his spine. Whit's low moans combined with the sound of skin slapping together was the most erotic thing he'd ever heard. His balls drew up tight.

As if sensing how close he was, Whit fisted Brody's cock in one hand and tweaked his nipple ring with the other, his hips thrusting up on each stroke. Brody flew, higher and higher, until he was calling Whit's name. His lover moved with him, carrying them over the peak together, and tumbling them down the other side until they fell against each other in a sweaty heap.

Rolling to their sides, they stayed pressed against each other, their hearts beating a staccato rhythm, breath coming in gasps as they fought for oxygen.

"So— Never— Can't—" Whit started and stopped several times.

"That supposed to be a sentence?" Brody questioned, then laughed softly and brushed the hair off his lover's damp forehead.

Whit shook his head, then the muscles in his face seemed to still, and Brody watched the doubt creep back. Whit took a deep breath and started over.

"Everything about what we just did felt right, Brody. Those weren't just words. I love you, and I want you with me…or me with you. I don't know how we do it, but say you meant it…say you'll stay."

Brody took his time in answering, savoring this moment, determined to capture the feelings so he could put them in a song. "I mean it, Whit. I've spent some time putting a few things in order. There's more to do, but I want to make the rest of those decisions together. I've been in Las Vegas the last couple of days, talking with a couple of casinos. I've been offered a couple of different gigs. One place wants to build me a show room, for fuck's sake." He shook his head at the absurdity of the idea.

"Yeah?" Whit said, his voice careful. "And what happens if they…you know…find out about us?"

"You know? *You know?*" Brody teased. Whit laughed, as he'd wanted him to. "Yeah, I know. And I already told both of them. Neither considers it any kind of a detriment to selling out shows. In fact Steve reminded me Las Vegas was home to Liberace long before gay was the latest cool cause."

Whit propped himself on his elbow and looked down at Brody. "What about Tim…and Lisa? What happened there?"

"Lisa has been pretty amazing, now that we've cleared the air. Tim paid her, you know? I don't suppose you watched the Today Show. Lisa stiffed them. Cancelled her appearance and said she'd been out of line. Of course that's just made the jackals hungrier for a story. Tim has tried to get me to change my mind non-stop, and insists he is the only one who can turn the story around—make it go away."

"And can he?"

"Hell no," Brody said. He lightly ran his finger along Whit's jawline. "This story has a life of its own—it's going to come out sooner or later, and I'd rather do it on my terms. Maybe in line with an announcement of what I'm gonna do next."

"Does that mean you're gonna do it? A regular show in Las Vegas instead of going on the road?"

"I don't know—wanted to talk to you. I did a little checking. Did you know there's another two thousand acres adjacent to your property that's for sale?"

"I can't afford that," Whit said. He started to rise, but Brody kept him in place.

"I can. Now don't start shaking your head before you hear me out. You want a ranch and I want privacy—and unless I entirely misunderstood what we just did here—we want each other. For the long haul."

Whit nodded once, his gaze fixed on Brody's face.

"Okay, so let's do it. Let's buy the land and design our place together. I might have money, but I don't know shit about starting a ranch. You know what needs to be done, but don't have much money. Is there anything wrong with wanting to pool our resources? It's what couples do all the time. We're equal partners each bringing our own assets, and we'll put all of it in both our names."

"Brody…honey… I don't know what to say. Your career, the singing, the shows—everyone would know."

"They practically know now—and I don't have to give up singing—but I don't have to live on the road anymore either. I can do a limited series of shows in Las Vegas without having to do the whole weekly concert routine. Or I could fill in for some of the regulars when their shows go dark. Besides, I want to ranch. I want to learn all these things I've been singing about. I want to write music. I can produce my own records when I'm ready.

"Right at this moment, I'm not tied to one single obligation. No tours, no record deal, nothing. Where I go next is up to me." He touched his fingers to Whit's lips. "And up to you. I love you, Whit. I want to stay here and build our home together. If you'll have me." He stopped talking then, wondering if he'd said too much, too soon.

Whit cupped the back of Brody's head, pulling him close, but not quite close enough to kiss. His eyes crinkled at the corners, and his breath was warm against Brody's lips. "If I'll have you? Forever won't be long enough," he said, echoing the words from Brody's song. "I'll be your home and you'll be mine."

Brody sang the words softly.

"Stay with me a while—forever won't be long enough.
"In my house, in my life, be my home.

"Invite me in…and never let me go away again."

~~The End~~

About the Author

Raised in California, Laura likes it hot, which explains why she ended up in Arizona via such diverse places as Japan, Maine, and Florida, and many more places in between. After retiring from the US Navy, she found a niche working for land management agencies, including the National Park Service and the Bureau of Land Management. Though she has held many jobs around the world, her favorite was working and living in Grand Canyon National Park. Working (and eating) in New Orleans was a close second. You will find many of her books are set against the rich backdrops provided by coastal Louisiana and northern Arizona.

When asked how she started writing, Laura tells of waking on Boxing Day a few years ago, with a woman named Elena MacFarland yammering in her dreams, demanding her story be told. Despite never attempting to write fiction before that morning, Laura ignored all of the holiday visitors and the Highland Destiny series was born. She doesn't believe it was a coincidence that the great grandmother who died when Laura was just a baby was named Elena MacFarland. Destiny does play a hand.

Laura became a full-time writer in 2012, and now she spends her time writing, watching her Arizona Diamondbacks, and working on her very own version of the Willow Springs Ranch in northwestern Arizona. She is a multi-published author of erotic romance, mystery, and urban fantasy and her books can be found at all major online retailers.

Connect with Laura at:

Twitter: *@LauraHarner*

Facebook: *facebook.com/lauraharner*

Or even better…check out the website at: *LauraHarner.com*

Also Available

~*~

Ty Hard, Willow Springs Ranch: 1

Tyler has used Don't Ask, Don't Tell as a shield against the truth since he was seventeen. Now, Ty finds himself cut loose from his Navy career after months of rehab from a debilitating head injury. At a loss as to what to do with his life, he travels to Willow Springs Ranch in Arizona to visit his surrogate father, only to arrive minutes after his oldest friend's death. Ty must come to terms with the loss while he fights to keep the PTSD from pulling him under. The last thing he's ready to think about is his growing attraction for another man.

Rancher Cass Cartwright's relationships never last more than a few hours, and that's just the way he likes it. Now he's in danger of doing the one thing he swore never to do: fall in love. Can Cass convince Ty to let go of his past or will sabotage at the ranch kill their love before it has a chance to grow?

~*~

Firestorm, Fighting Fire: 1

When a wildland fire lands Scott McGregor in the burn unit and sends his career up in smoke, a decade-old emergency contact card brings his former college lover, Robby Hammond, to his hospital bed. After six months of hospitals and rehab, Scott starts a new life as owner of the Mountain Shadows Campground. Maybe learning to run a bed and breakfast—not to mention dealing with the permanent residents—will keep him from making Robby the center of his universe. *Again.*

Leaving San Francisco to take a part-time position as a law enforcement ranger makes no sense at this stage of his life, but after Scott's critical burns, Robby moves to Flagstaff anyway—to take up residence at Mountain Shadows—which has nothing to do with his long-buried feelings for his ex. Despite the white-hot attraction that still burns between them, too much is at stake for Robby to take that chance. Again.

Torn apart a dozen years ago by an unlimited ability to cause each other pain, each man believes the relationship door is firmly closed, but when life brings them back together, Scott is still the irresistible force to Robby's immovable object, and where there's smoke…there's fire.

~*~

Continental Divide, Separate Ways: 1

Detective Remington frickin' hates the missing persons detail, but a cold fury builds in the pit of his stomach when he realizes that over the past three months six boys have disappeared from the smaller communities that surround the greater Phoenix area. All reported to be runaways looking to escape their shitty lives, but Remy's starting to put together a different picture and he doesn't like it one damn bit.

Inspector Jamie Mainwaring stares at the six reports, willing them to make sense. Six boys, six months, all from just outside of London, which meant six different investigations. All of the boys were between the ages of ten and fifteen, all purportedly runaways from dysfunctional families. Something was rotten in Denmark.

There are always runaways. Every small town loses them--every big city collects them. Kids look for freedom and discover they have more to lose than they ever thought possible. London and Phoenix, culture and cowboys, nothing linking these two sprawling metropolitan areas. Nothing except a hit on a computer data search.

Two cops, one a cowboy, the other a Lord. A secret government agency, human trafficking, and a blazing hot mutual distraction.

This is the first installment in the Separate Ways Series. The books should be enjoyed in the following order:

~*~

Oceans Apart, Separate Ways: 2

It's been two years since Lord Jamie Mainwaring and Detective Remy Remington worked and loved their way through their one and only case before going their separate ways.

Now Jamie is once again mixing agency business with pleasure as he and his partner, Agent Ryan Whiteside, are assigned to a case involving piracy in the Caribbean.

Remy and his old friend Miggy are still detectives, but they've gone private in Phoenix. When their biggest client sends them to supervise an unusual diamond transfer, they think their toughest challenge will be maintaining their cover as a gay couple on a barefoot-style cruise.

When murder connects the dots between the two cases, the four men must learn to work together as relationships and loyalties are tested amid misunderstandings and memories on the high seas.

~*~

Moving Mountains, Separate Ways: 3

It's easier to move a mountain than escape the past.

After the ultimate betrayal results in the death of his lover, Jamie Mainwaring looks to the past for answers, and discovers his entire life is a lie. When uncovering the truth leads to a more devastating loss, there's only one place he can turn for understanding.

When former-detective Remington left the police department, he never looked back. Now, his glory-stealing ex-boss is dead, leaving Remy's real name scratched in the dirt at the brutal murder scene.

Two years ago, Miguel Rojas left New York in the back of his best friend's car, in real danger of falling victim to the same addictions that left his twin sister in bed with the drug lord he'd been deep undercover investigating. When she shows up looking to make amends, misplaced guilt mixed with curiosity open old wounds.

While Remy returns to his police department roots to track down a killer, Miggy and Jamie team up to find the bones from Miggy's past and bury them once and for all.

The truth shall set you free—except when the past is determined to claim you.

~*~

Prevailing Winds, Separate Ways: 4

Two years ago, Jamie Mainwaring and Remy Remington had nothing in common except missing boys and a blazing hot mutual distraction. When the case was over, so were they. Although they went their separate ways, life—and death—keep the men connected.

After another deadly tragedy touches both their lives, the men say what they believe must be their final goodbyes—only to have their worlds collide once again. This time they end up in Las Vegas, one man for work, the other to try to mend a very personal pain.

Although Jamie and Remy once excelled at mixing business with pleasure—this time, the stakes are much higher—they've got forever on the line. When they discover Jamie's case has an unexpected connection to Remy's son, they must put everything aside to find Toby before the young man makes a decision that will change all of their lives. One thing is positive, time is running out.

www.ingramcontent.com/pod-product-compliance
Lightning Source LLC
Chambersburg PA
CBHW030255130626
46549CB00002B/536